PERIODIC EAST

Book One

Gabriel L. Rodríguez

INDIE EARTH
PUBLISHING

PERIODIC EAST

Book One

Gabriel L. Rodríguez

"If there's a book you really want to read but it hasn't been written yet, then you must write it."

— TONI MORRISON

*To my mother, who was the first person
to tell me I was a "fucking writer."*

"If man is to survive, he will have learned to take a delight in the essential differences between men and between cultures. He will learn that differences in ideas and attitudes are a delight, part of life's exciting variety, not something to fear."

— **GENE RODDENBERRY**

THE NEW ICE AGE

It had been six years since The Blast and every day since had been a nightmare. Mother Nature was on life support and Nuclear Winter had set in. All forms of fossil fuels, and most energy sources, were depleted to zero and many citizens of the world died clenching their loved ones or clenching their pearls. Governments turned into a free-for-all and world economies took their final swan dive into oblivion. This troubled, but lively planet that—at one point—was home to almost eight billion people dwindled down to what we, the survivors, assumed was under one hundred thousand, but I was sure more died with the cold and harsh conditions.

Most of the survivors migrated to one of two main areas. I was able to make my way south from Louisiana all the way to what was once known as the Amazon Rainforest. The area offered an ample amount of food and shelter.

The weather took getting used to. Even though the radiation didn't reach where we set up camp, The Blast had already done its work.

One of the survivors in our camp, a clever kid, had dug up an old thermometer and got it working. The highest the temperature had reached since we arrived was ten degrees Fahrenheit.

We were in the New Ice Age. Every body of water on the planet was frozen solid, and boats and other water vehicles were used primarily as shelters—the gas in the engines siphoned dry long ago.

Communication was tricky, at best. Our satellites were still orbiting around us in what we assumed was working order, but the technology to communicate with them didn't survive. Or, at least, no one who knew how to communicate with the technology that had survived.

We knew that First Contact was made either soon before or soon after The Blast, but there was no way to know if the aliens caused the global downfall, or if it was just a few dirty bombs launched from a handful of countries run by egomaniacal sociopaths. Either way, First Contact was the only contact we had—if it had even happened at all—and after the world froze over, the aliens never contacted us again. If they had, we had no way of knowing.

ONE

My job was simple: keep everyone in my camp alive. I volunteered half-jokingly when the first of us arrived. That was four years ago, but it had become easy. To govern. To lead. People didn't care about things like race, status, and wealth like they did before. All that mattered was community and surviving. No one wanted to be the last person on Earth. The thought of that gave many of the survivors nightmares, myself included.

I lived on a sailboat locked into the frozen ocean about two hundred yards from land, but it was all "land" now, to an extent. The cabin doors kept freezing shut, so I had replaced them with thermal "sails" I had sewn together from a few dozen pairs of thermal underwear.

I was awoken by good news. Two young polar bears had been killed and were being skinned for their hide and prepped for consumption.

My camp consisted of just under forty people, last counted just a few days before. People would come and go as they pleased, but it happened less frequently. Usually, someone would join or leave camp because they had found a loved one thought killed in The Blast, but it had been a year since the last time that happened.

It was a beautiful day outside. The sky was so clear it was nearly identical in color to the frozen ground. It was so clear, in fact, you could see Icarus, the satellite that—rumor had it—intercepted the First Contact transmission. Icarus stuck out like a burnt pixel in an otherwise flawless plasma TV screen.

Icarus had launched about ten years before. At least, it had been ten years when everyone noticed it and NASA made an official announcement. Most of us thought it launched way before and everyone was too distracted with everything else. It took the "official" end of World War III, after six countries were nuked into a crater, for everyone to decide to… just… stop.

Icarus also served as a space station; a huge one. It was reported that seventy-four people lived on board. The war had been going on for so long and with no end in sight. NASA and world leaders bankrupted themselves so their best and brightest could build a space station large enough to get people to Mars and finally colonize the damn thing. In the most desperate of circumstances, world leaders recruited their best and brightest candidates to win a spot on Icarus. Doctors, artists, politicians, scientists, laborers; every kind of person you would need—but only the absolute best of each.

As I understood it—and I don't think I fully did— NASA claimed that Mars would be ready to easily sustain human life within days of Icarus arriving in the planet's orbit. How? They took three nuclear warheads, each one the size of a school bus, with them. They were to be launched targeting each pole in order to rapidly accelerate the Greenhouse Gas Effect to remove all the toxic chemicals in the Mars atmosphere.

I didn't know if Icarus ever left our line of sight, if it went to Mars and their idea didn't work or if they went and decided to come back and ominously loom over us as we all froze and starved to death for the fun of it.

As I made my way to camp, I was greeted by Sara, the same little girl who had told me about the polar bears. Sara had bright blue eyes and long, strawberry blonde hair. She was curled up next to the great fire at the center of camp where the bear meat was cooking. The smell of the polar bear was gamey, almost like a roasted gator from back home, but not really.

The little girl was with her brother, Miles, who was much older than her. Miles stood over six feet and had the same eyes as Sara. They had lost their parents in The Blast, and soon stumbled into the camp several months after I had. Miles had arrived battling frostbite, hypothermia, dehydration, and starvation. He was also carrying a giant backpack that I thought was filled with supplies, but all he was actually carrying in his backpack was Sara, somehow managing to keep her warm and alive.

"Look, Miles," she said excitedly. "Tiberius is here."

"I see him, Sara."

He stood slowly and saluted me. I hated that he did that each morning. I insisted that he didn't have to, but it would upset him. Soon after, I realized that it was better to just allow the few seconds of awkwardness each morning and not make things weirder for either of us.

"Good morning, sir!" he bellowed.

"Good morning, Miles."

Miles was in his late thirties, and a lieutenant in the first-ever assembled Planetary Advancement of Geographic Exploration Sciences (PAGES). Before that, he was an elite soldier in the South African military.

PAGES was supposed to be a privately funded space program. As NASA lost control of their finances, a group of eccentric billionaires believed the program was necessary to speed up the necessity of terraforming other planetary bodies, especially with the ever-looming threat of nuclear war and accelerated climate change. But once NASA went bankrupt with the creation of Icarus and funding stopped because of World War III, the world knew we couldn't survive on the planet for much longer, despite PAGES.

The top one percent of the top one percent became homeless literally overnight thinking they could buy themselves the first ticket off the planet in order to survive. All efforts were futile for several reasons. Some more obvious than others.

So, there I was. There we all were. Minus eighteen degrees in the Brazilian Amazon, at least relieved—or maybe cursed—that we got to live another day. Like this.

✦

I sat next to Miles and we both looked up at Icarus.

"So close, yet so far," Miles said. "I almost feel like if I had a rugby ball and I threw it up in the air, I could reach it."

"If only," I replied.

"No word from anyone new, right?"

Miles would ask me this every morning like clockwork. His tone was always the same. Already knowing the answer and wanting me to lie. I never did. That would make things worse. Like if my answers were keeping his sanity intact.

"No word, Miles."

Sara was rotating the meat on a frozen tree branch. A small iron pot of newly boiled water was quickly cooling. The makeshift kitchen was very bare bones, but still very efficient.

"Want some coffee, Tiberius? The bear is almost ready," she spoke with an excited tone; so proud in knowing that, at her young age, what she did in camp was crucial to our survival and she never faltered at it.

"Thank you, Sara, I can get it. Just keep an eye on the meat so it doesn't overcook."

"Yes, sir," she exclaimed excitedly.

I smiled, served myself some coffee, and made my morning rounds. Pretty much everyone in my camp was already awake. There hadn't been a major illness or injury in months, and for that we were all extremely lucky. I made my way to the end of camp about two hundred yards from the location of the fire. There was a huge tent that belonged and was home to Daniel, the oldest in the camp. At eighty-four, he was the oldest by over thirty years of anyone else. He often boasted that he was the oldest person left on Earth, and he was probably right.

Daniel was from Bilbao, which I learned was a region between Spain and France. His English wasn't very good, but he tried. I made a respective effort to communicate with him in Spanish; one of the many languages he spoke. I had mastered formal introductions, but beyond that, not so much.

"Good morning, Tiberius," he said, his accent very thick.

"*Buenos días,*" I replied. "How are you feeling today?"

"Older dan yesterday."

I smiled. I had an appreciation for his kind of dorky dad sense of humor.

"There is fresh polar bear. It should be ready soon."

"Ah, *gracias.* Thank you, *comandante,*" he replied. The appreciation in his tone was clear.

"*Comandante?*" I asked.

He looked around as if he were hoping to find the translation in the frosty air. I repeated the word a few times to myself and soon realized what it meant.

"Commander?"

"*Sí.*"

"No, Daniel. No *comandante.* Just Tiberius."

"But you are boss. You are *súper comandante.*"

He stood up from his folding chair recliner, his knees cracking. Then, he saluted me. Just like Miles would. I saluted him back. A man who has lived the life Daniel has for as long as he has deserved it. Daniel was on a ship when The Blast hapened. The ship I lived on, in fact. He had refused to live in it after I arrived and was voted camp leader despite my protest, which turned out to be futile.

"*El comandante debe vivir en una habitación para comandantes*," he preached. I learned it meant that a commander must live in a proper commander's quarters.

The adjustment of culture and anthropology as a whole had been new to everyone. Those who wouldn't accept it or couldn't adapt died soon after.

Language in particular went through quite a change. The world was both smaller and bigger than ever, but even before The Blast, something historic happened. The United Nations met to negotiate a deal, the deal of language.

With so few people left in the world, an attempt was made to initiate a one-world government. Something that was dismissed almost as quickly as it was proposed. But in the midst of the failed attempts, one former government leader had made a bold claim; that a transmission had been received from an unknown source in a language that hadn't been formally spoken for over a century.

Later, some dark web sleuths and linguists were steadfast in confirming that the language spoken was Basque. This was another reason why Daniel was so important. He was one of the last people left on the planet—if not *the* last—that spoke it fluently. We never knew for sure if this transmission was from an alien creature, and as far as I knew, nobody did. But knowing that Daniel spoke the language gave everyone an unexplained sense of relief.

Daniel also spoke French, Italian, and Catalan. But alas, no one else in our camp spoke any of those languages. Miles and Sara spoke Afrikaans. There were sisters in the camp that spoke Dutch, so Sara and Miles were able to communicate with them in their native tongue for the most part, which was nice. And there had been a small boy from Japan when I arrived. Sadly, he froze to death a few days later.

The geographic part of the world that was believed to have the most survivors at the time of The Blast was the southern tip of Argentina, near the South Pole. But those survivors migrated east on a giant ferry before Nuclear Winter set in. I didn't know how many survived or where they went.

After speaking to Daniel for a few more minutes, I continued with my rounds, but was stopped in my tracks by… tracks. The plushy snow showed a heavy imprint of a single footprint. It was slightly larger than my own footprint. However, it was a *bare* foot. That was suicide in the Nuclear Winter. A person would get frostbite in seconds if they buried their feet in the snow. It also seemed to have an extra-long toe sticking out of the right side.

Could it have been a print from an alien? The odds of this were slim to none. But still slim. It was likely a birth defect or a mutation. Mutations as a result of overexposure to radiation in some survivors were common, but after six years, most survivors that had mutations as a result of prolonged exposure were believed to have all died out. I guess it was possible to still have some survivors with mutations, but, understandably, they would do everything in their power to not reveal them to anyone. Besides that, what we assumed was First Contact with another intellectual species was through sound. We had no idea what they looked like. We never got a chance to ask.

After staring at the print for an extra minute or two, I convinced myself that it was just a regular footprint done from one of the teenagers on a stupid dare and they stepped on a branch that was buried in the snow.

By the time I got back to the center of camp, most people were already eating breakfast. A chunk of bear meat was set aside for me along with boiled plantain leaves and some reserved chocolate mini bars.

"Everyone doing well today?" I asked.

The camp quietly nodded almost in unison.

"Any news or concerns?"

Everyone looked at each other almost suggesting that they all knew something that I didn't.

"What is it?" I pried. "If something is bothering you, please tell me. I promise I won't get mad."

The survivors stared at each other again in silence, waiting to see who would speak first. I started to worry.

Then, I heard a voice say, "I made contact."

TWO

The people in the camp showed a unified false sense of surprise. The voice that spoke was Joshua, a petulant child in a forty-year-old body.

"When did you make contact, Joshua?" I asked, my tone trying to remain calm and a little doubtful.

"I made contact yesterday. I told you I did."

"No, you didn't."

"I did. You just weren't paying attention. Again. Some leader you're turning out to be…"

"Hey!" Miles immediately shouted, startling Sara.

I put my arm up slowly to calm him down. Miles was looking over at Joshua ready to pounce.

"What kind of contact did you make, Joshua?"

"Direct," he answered dryly. "I saw one of them."

To that, everyone reacted with genuine shock. Including me. I quickly quieted the loud murmurs of the camp and started walking towards him.

He met me halfway.

"You saw one of them. Are you sure?" I asked in a lower voice.

"Of course, I'm sure. Like I told you yesterday. Remember? Oh wait… you don't."

The arrogance of that man.

"Why don't you tell me what happened? From the beginning."

I quickly sipped my coffee as Joshua made his declaration. He had the floor.

"I was deep in the Ice Jungle. I was gathering provisions that I could chisel out of the ice."

"Did you find anything good?" I asked, genuinely curious. No one in camp had found anything significant in weeks, but the Ice Jungle was massive. We knew there was more to discover and thaw out of the ice.

"Of course. How else do you think I made contact?" Joshua exclaimed.

Everyone stopped eating and sipping their coffee. Loud murmurs quickly became more coherent. I immediately turned towards the camp to try to quiet them down so that Joshua could finish what he had to say. Once they quieted down, I turned towards Joshua and walked within a foot of where he stood.

"Are you saying that you found a frozen… alien… body… within walking distance of camp?"

"Well, he's not frozen anymore. I dug him out."

Rage suddenly washed over my face while confusion, fear, and anger swept across the faces of everyone else in the camp.

"Is he conscious?" I asked.

"Of course not," Joshua scoffed.

"Exactly how far off from camp was this?"

"Less than two klicks east, southeast."

I looked to Miles to translate the military lexicon. Joshua had also served in the US Army—dishonorably discharged, I later found out, but I didn't know why. According to Joshua, he served for two years, but never told me where he served or what his final rank was before being discharged.

"Two kilometers," Miles said. Just under a mile and a

half for my non-metric system-adapting American self.

"Alright, Joshua," I began. "Show me."

Joshua smirked his usual condescending smirk but nodded. The survivors looked on in worried confusion as I addressed them.

"I'm sure there's nothing to be worried about. Joshua and I will return soon. Please continue your duties and remain close to camp until we return."

"I'm going with you," Miles interjected, sheathing his machete.

I could tell by his tone that he wasn't asking. Sara wanted to come along, but Miles discretely shooed her away and she begrudgingly obeyed, staying back with Daniel and the others.

"We will *all* be back soon," I said as the three of us vanished into the Ice Jungle.

THREE

The Ice Jungle was hauntingly beautiful. As if a polaroid was in its first bleach-white stage of development and stayed that way. Everything had been flash-frozen and perfectly preserved. This was why food was not in short supply. But you had to work for it.

A piece of fruit took a minimum of one hour to thaw out of its ice sarcophagus and prepare; one piece. This was why the camp had an eighteen-hours-per-day three-person rotation for food. Shifts were divided into three categories: gathering, thawing, and preparing. There were a few pieces of frozen fruit and large animals that Miles was often easily able to chisel out of the ground, always with the intention of taking them back to camp.

Joshua walked ahead of us in a silent fervor. If this alien body really was less than two klicks away like he had claimed, we should've already reached it.

"Lost?" Miles asked confrontationally.

"Of course not," Joshua replied with hesitation in his voice. "It's just past these palms. I recognize the one with the recently thawed branch."

He pressed forward and we followed closely. After a few yards, he stopped and pointed to a wide, shallow hole in the ground.

"Where is it?" Miles asked.

"It… was here," Joshua answered as he checked his

surroundings quickly. "It was right here," he repeated with more certainty.

"*Was*?" I contested.

"What did it look like?" Miles asked as I observed him transitioning into soldier mode while he reached for his machete.

I found myself still staring at what I perceived was a shallow grave, only it wasn't a grave anymore, just a shallow hole. The powdery snow had an imprint that something had been there—there was no doubt about that. After looking around some more, I came across a footprint. Then another. It had the exact same shape as the track I had seen. The one that looked like an enlarged human foot only with what appeared to be an extra long dislocated toe. Within a few steps, I discovered a clear track of several footprints.

"Miles, Joshua," I started. "We should get back to camp, make sure everyone is safe, and formulate a plan."

"Agreed," Miles whispered as I noticed his defensive stance getting lower.

"Joshua, do you have a different opinion?" I asked, but the bastard didn't respond. "Joshua," I called out again in a loud whisper, but he had vanished.

"Where did he go? I didn't see or hear any movement," Miles said.

"Maybe he just headed back to camp on his own," I stipulated.

"We should head back to camp, Tiberius," Miles said.

"Agreed, but we need to be sure that Joshua—"

Suddenly, we heard a blood-curdling scream. Miles instinctively ran in the direction of the sound. After a few yards of him slicing through the frozen bush, he suddenly stopped. I trailed a few steps behind, coming to an abrupt halt next to him.

We were both looking down on the blankety snow where a decapitated Joshua lay. His blood was already frozen over and unable to gush out.

Miles looked around frantically for a sign of the alien; another track, an unfamiliar sound, Joshua's head. But there was nothing immediately noticeable. All I could do was stand perfectly still staring at Joshua's headless body.

I had seen a few dead bodies since The Blast. A few had even died in my arms, but never had I seen this.

Miles had. Miles had seen much worse. Miles didn't even flinch as I cupped my hands over my face.

"Miles," I whispered. "We need to get back to camp and warn the others. We need to relocate. Tonight."

Miles nodded in agreement without making a sound. We walked back-to-back rotating three-hundred-sixty degrees for about a quarter mile before we both just turned and sprinted towards camp.

By the time we made it back, it was nearly nightfall. Sara happily ran over to Miles and he immediately picked her up and hugged her tight. I was greeted by Daniel and a few of the other survivors.

"I need you to gather everyone," I told them. "Even the children. I have something of extreme importance to discuss."

"Where is Joshua?" one of the survivors asked.

"Please," I stated, "gather everyone. There's been a tragedy."

The women immediately scurried off and started to gather everyone.

Within minutes, every member of the camp was huddled around the large fire. Some were quietly awaiting instruction while sipping tea. The younger and more anxious ones had already started whispering gossip to each other. Miles was standing by my side with Sara clenched tightly to his waist. On my other side was Daniel. He was seated on a large, padded folding chair.

As the murmurs grew softer and all the members of the camp settled into their chairs, I stepped forward and raised my arms for silence like a conductor addressing his orchestra.

"Everyone," I began. Even that first word brought out a quiver in my voice. I quickly cleared my throat and continued. "Earlier today, Miles, Joshua, and I went into the Ice Jungle to find something Joshua had claimed to have seen."

"Was it an alien? It's out there, isn't it? We're all going to die!" a woman shouted.

"Where is Joshua?" shouted another.

The murmurs started again.

"Joshua has been killed," I shouted over the drowning voices. It had come out quite insensitive, but it wasn't the time for me to worry about that. I had started an all-out panic.

It wasn't until that moment that I began to understand the mess we were all in. We wouldn't be able to relocate safely, especially without a proper plan. But we couldn't stay put either. It was too dangerous, especially since Miles and I knew what was out there. At least we thought we knew.

"We have to make a decision," I announced. "And we need to make it now." The camp grew silent. "The closest known neighboring camp is seventy miles southeast of here. Here are your options: you can join me as I make my way there, taking only what you absolutely need. You can go your own way and try to establish a new camp somewhere else. Or if you prefer, you can stay here."

Daniel stood after I finished speaking. "I go with you," he said in his broken English.

I nodded and looked out to the rest of the camp. The survivors seemed divided over what they wanted to do. Children were crying and arguing with their parents—they were the luckiest of all; entire families who had survived The Blast.

Sara squeezed Miles's hand. "What are we going to do, Miles?" I heard her say.

Miles exhaled.

"Miles," she repeated.

He looked down at Sara and knelt down to meet her eyes.

"Sara," he began. "What do you want to do?"

Sara seemed almost confused by the question, but then she quickly said, "Maybe the aliens will know what we should do. Can we ask them?"

Miles looked up at me expecting a logical answer to Sara's question instead I turned my attention to the other survivors.

"I will gather my belongings. Those who want to join me, I will be back here in thirty minutes. For those who don't, there are no hard feelings and it has been an honor to have been in your company."

I took a deep breath and stared at their bewildered and terrified faces. I flashed a nervous grin and started walking towards the boat I had lived in since I had arrived, knowing that it would be the last time I would see the inside of it.

FOUR

I was surprised by how many possessions I actually had. A few changes of clothes, a sleeping bag, an old lantern, and some personal items. Still, I was able to fit it all in my pack easily. When I stepped out of the ship and gingerly made my way across the ice, I saw only a few people waiting for me.

I was a little surprised. I noticed as I walked over that some people had already left on their own while others, I could see, had no intent on leaving. Along with Daniel, Miles, and Sara, there were about a dozen men and women ranging from the ages of seven to fifty.

"Is this everyone?" I asked. Everyone nodded silently. It was understandable that all of them—even Miles—had a look of anxiety, doubt, and adrenaline. I smiled and took a deep breath.

"Okay. How much food do we have with us?"

One of the young women raised her bag and said, "I have this filled with banana leaves, chocolate bar reserves, and some plantains. Should be enough for all of us for the next few days."

That was more than enough. We all knew how to find and forage food, but my most obvious concern was encountering that alien, or whatever it was, that killed Joshua.

Another young woman who rarely spoke to me while in the camp stepped forward. She wore a large polar bear pelt that camouflaged her perfectly and spoke with a thick accent.

"Tiberius, I would like to volunteer to lead this group and take the first watch for the night when we stop to rest."

Miles looked at me and shrugged his shoulders as the woman disappeared into her giant pelt.

"You do?" I asked, almost relieved.

"Forgive me!" she shouted unnecessarily and then quickly adjusted her volume. "I don't mean to challenge your authority."

I smiled. "When did I ever have authority over anyone?"

She looked at me terrified. I guess they didn't have rhetorical questions where she came from. I stepped aside and extended my arm. "Everyone," I began. "We will follow," I leaned in to be reminded of her name.

"Ada," she responded.

"We will follow Ada southeast toward the nearest known camp."

Ada smiled nervously and stepped forward. She turned towards the small group.

"I will find us a suitable new home," she began. "I promise."

She certainly sounded like a leader.

Within an hour, Sara was already complaining to Miles that she was tired of walking. Ada tried to ignore her and pressed on. Miles picked her up and made his way next to me.

"I've talked to her a few times before," he began. "She lost a child about Sara's age in The Blast. In fact, according to her, she looked just like Sara."

A few minutes later, we came across a massive tree. Its trunk must've been fifteen feet round and if you were to climb to the top, you'd feel as if you could touch Icarus.

"Ada," I said, "I think it would be a good idea for us to

rest here. We can prepare more water and excavate for food and supplies."

Reluctantly, Ada held up a fist, her arm at a ninety-degree angle.

"We'll rest here for a moment. Prepare water and excavate the area, but stay close. I don't want anyone to get separated from the group."

"Thank you, Ada," I said.

The tree really was something. Some of the members of the group were placing bets and bragging over who'd be able to climb to the top the fastest or who would've been able to cut it down first under normal conditions. The sun's reflection on the frozen tree gave it a golden glow. The only vibrant color anyone saw anymore came from the sun when it reflected off certain foliage.

The temperature was starting to drop again.

Ada suddenly shouted, "It's too cold to continue on today. We'll set up camp here for tonight."

No doubt some sound wisdom from Miles, accompanied by Sara's complaining, helped Ada reach that decision.

FIVE

A mere two hundred fifty kilometers above in the sky, just past the thermosphere, was the space station and spaceship Icarus. She had been "floating" her slim three-hundred-ton frame it seemed like forever—her "floating" made possible by a very convenient combination of circumstances.

The gravitational pulls from the artificially created black holes served as tethers for each major hemisphere of Icarus. It was essentially the hammock ties. The sun, naturally, provided all the energy the station would ever need. All seventy-four original members—plus three new additions—were accounted for. Healthy. Thriving.

Icarus was a paradise, leaps and bounds beyond what the greatest places on Earth once were before The Blast.

The supercomputer that ran Icarus on its own was just finishing another self-diagnostic test. Seventy trillion lines of code, procedures, inventory, bio-readings, and more were completed in forty-four hundredths of a second. You'd never even notice it. It was called the Symbiotic Icarus System. The crew referred to it as SIS.

Dr. Kairi Miyaki woke up to her hologram alarm clock playing a concerto of Sakai's third movement in E minor. She enjoyed waking up to the tones of classical music. At the age of twenty-seven, Kairi was the only person on board with any hands-on maintenance with SIS. That was because Kairi designed and programmed SIS from scratch as a "side project" and completed the first prototype when she was eleven. NASA had taken notice and immediately offered her a job. Kairi was an example of the type of people that NASA and the top one percent of the top one percent funded to save.

Her quarters on Icarus were located on the southeast end of the ship. In her bed, she wasn't alone and she had nearly forgotten that.

Sam rolled his small but muscular frame over to spoon Kairi, but she would have nothing of it. She quickly sat up and reached for her silk robe that really covered nothing.

"Good morning, SIS," she said.

A few muted clicks sounded in response and a gigantic see-through touch screen appeared on one of her bare walls.

"Good morning, Kairi," it returned.

SIS's voice response could be modified to any user's preference from a vast sound library of artists, celebrities, historical figures, and a few hundred thousand family members and friends of the crew for good measure. For Kairi, the voice that responded to her was a default robotic-sounding voice with a slight accent from what was once Northern Ireland.

Of the original seventy-four person crew, sixty-eight were American-born or American citizens. Kairi was one of the other original six originating from other countries.

The only child of Yuki and Hiroto Miyaki—Japanese diplomats from the Nagasaki prefecture who immigrated to Argentina before their daughter was born—Kairi came into the world surrounded by a plethora of culture and privilege. It was a delicate tightrope she walked to rebel against, but never took for granted.

Being sent to the best international schools, Kairi spent her formative years being educated in English and Spanish at school and then in Japanese at home by her parents.

An exceedingly gifted child, she skipped multiple levels in school, quickly leaving her classmates behind. Though she tried to be a regular kid despite her genius, the other children felt threatened and often abandoned her. Despite this, she took it upon herself to familiarize and embrace the Eastern, Western, and Latin cultures on her own, often simultaneously. One way she achieved this was by putting chimichurri, a specialized Argentine sauce, on her sushi rolls at dinner instead of wasabi while watching archaic American cult classics of the nineties such as *Unsolved Mysteries*. Kairi's parents were… conflicted, to say the least, when it came to her customized menu at the dinner table. They wanted their daughter to express herself as any normal kid would, but they also didn't want for her to do anything that would besmirch or disrespect their ancient cultures and traditions, or the culture of the new land they now called home.

Upon tasting the culinary fusion themselves, Kairi's father, who tasted it first, had a visceral reaction to it. An expression of too much grease and unfamiliar herbs on top of a flawless piece of salty uni. To Hiroto, the Japanese-Argentine fusion tasted abhorrent. Kairi's mother, however, thought it was the best thing she ever tasted, but refused to say so after seeing her husband's reaction. Yuki would later sneak midnight snacks of uni with chimichurri for years before Hiroto ever found out. One fateful night after an unfortunate reaction to a dairy-soaked beverage before bed was when he made his discovery. It turned out that, due to the food poisoning, Hiroto's recollection of it was closer interpreted as a fever dream than it actually happening. Yuki never corrected him and they never discussed it.

The dinner table was the only place where the Miyaki family gathered regularly. It was at the dinner table that they realized the extent of their daughter's genius; particularly in computer science, engineering, and the culinary arts.

Though Kairi refused to take an IQ test, experts believed her IQ was over two hundred. Stephen Hawking and Albert Einstein each had an IQ of one hundred sixty, easily making Kairi the smartest person on the planet when she lived on one.

"Come back to bed," Sam pleaded, his face half covered by the blankets.

"Why are you still here?" she protested.

"I thought—"

"That was your first mistake."

"Can I at least get you some breakfast? Make sure you still eat; that you're still human?"

"No."

Sam sat up in the bed and rubbed his eyes. He ran his fingers through his thick, golden hair. Reaching for his boxers and sliding them on, he looked back at Kairi and said, "You're a fucking bitch."

He grabbed the rest of his things and walked out.

Kairi didn't even flinch.

SIX

Sam was angry; angrier than he thought he would be. He walked across the ample hallways of Icarus at a rapid pace. Each step louder than the last echoed across the hall at the hour of 5:45 AM Earth's EST, which was the timezone Icarus operated on.

His quarters were located on the northeast wing; a lengthy eight-minute walk from Kairi's. As Sam placed his handprint over a panel next to his door to unlock it, SIS greeted him with its own custom voice to Sam's preference.

"Good morning, Sam."

"Don't talk to me!" Sam shouted. A few muted clicks later, you couldn't hear a sound.

Sam's quarters were decorated like that of a wannabe frat boy hiding his own genius. Abstract paintings decorated his walls along with an old-fashioned paper poster of a Sports Illustrated swimsuit model circa 1997.

A bookshelf with some classic comic books was overshadowed by several more books on abnormal psychology, forensic sciences, hydroelectric engineering, theoretical physics, and particle physics.

His furniture was very bare bones and simple in appearance but was obviously capable of climate control, vibration, and even had a built-in projector.

He went to the far wall of his quarters to another touchscreen console. He punched in a few commands and, all of the sudden, a door inside his quarters made a *swoosh* sound as it opened and Sam could hear a cascade of water start to rain down from the shower head. Showers were Sam's escape. The longer the shower, the longer he needed his escape.

This one would take a while.

Even though this was his first time sleeping with Kairi, Sam had hoped that she would not take it as a one-night stand. Sam had *worked* for this. He had tried to impress her. Woo her. Court her. Weeks of planning and changed plans turned into more weeks of more planning and changed plans, and in the end, it seemed to have been for nothing.

She had done a great job, the night before, of convincing him that something had changed, that there had been some sort of spark between them.

Sam had first met Kairi in the most formal of settings, during his final interview that determined if he was to be placed on Icarus. He remembered it both fondly and angrily as the hot water cascaded over him. Sam's final interview—like every member on Icarus—consisted of an abundance of questions after days worth of personality and IQ tests, followed by hours worth of scrutinizing questions from the results of those personality and IQ tests.

As the interview was finally winding down, Captain Katherine Bellamy and Dr. Kairi Miyaki asked their final questions.

Captain Bellamy's question was, "What do you hope for Icarus and its crew to accomplish?"

Sam answered honestly and his answer was simple yet effective.

"I hope it will become the start of a new history," he began. "A new Renaissance of progress, discovery, and evolution that will thrive and pale by comparison to the first Renaissance."

Sam noticed Kairi's smile as she tried to hide her face

behind the digital pad with his profile and biological signatures. Then, she made eye contact with him and smiled again; something that she had been infamous for *not* doing throughout any other interview whether the candidate was selected as a member of the crew or not. Sam was trying not to allow himself to get too excited over seeing Dr. Kairi Miyaki's contagious but rarely shown smile. He didn't want it to raise any red flags in his bio-readings. But it was obvious that Sam had quickly become quite smitten with her.

After gathering herself, Dr. Kairi Miyaki asked her own question. A real curveball.

"How would you plan a romantic outing onboard Icarus?"

Sam didn't know if this is what she had asked all the candidates or if it was a question just for him. All he knew for certain was that every candidate, male or female, received a question meant to toy with their emotions.

He took a deep breath, but not too deep to suggest anxiety or uncertainty. He discreetly slid his palms over his thighs to cover the clammy sweat. These rooms were always too hot or too cold, he thought.

"With you?" Sam blurted out.

Captain Bellamy raised an eyebrow at the initial response.

"Or in general, Mr. Ng," Captain Bellamy interjected.

"I see," Sam replied. "Ashes to ashes and dust to dust. At least that's what we're led to believe. The universe is so vast that the light from those who we've lost cannot reach every part of the universe in a single instant. So, at some point, somewhere, who we were and what we were and how we lived… that light will reach a new part of the universe. Why can't that apply to us? I'd like to imagine that, on a romantic outing on Icarus, we could relive moments in our lives by looking out and being reminded of who we were, who we are, and who we could be."

Dr. Kairi Miyaki leaned back in her chair slightly and discretely waved off her strands of hair that had managed to break free from tightly wound bun. Her speech even had the slightest hesitation, Sam remembered, when she responded.

"Thank—thank you, Mr. Ng. This concludes your final interview. You will have our decision soon. There is nothing more you need to do until that time," she had said with a playful smile.

Letting the steaming hot water soak his skin, Sam was determined to not let his emotions get the better of him ever again. He wanted to make Kairi suffer emotionally. He just needed to figure out how to make that happen.

SEVEN

The cold was a dangerous and powerful deterrent. Ada hadn't thought about her decision to volunteer as a leader all the way through. Being a leader meant that she needed to stay outside to keep watch.

I could see her from my thermal tent with her hands placed over the makeshift fire that did little to prevent oncoming hypothermia. She was shivering like a maraca being played by a drunken mariachi. I felt I had no other choice but to relieve her and come outside myself.

"I'll take your shift," I said. "I insist."

Ada nodded in thanks and immediately retreated to her tent. She didn't need any additional convincing.

The snow was coming down hard. Even though the camp only moved a few miles, we felt the piercing cold stab through our pelts like a finely sharpened blade in ways I hadn't experienced in a long time. It was not only dangerously cold, it was deathly cold.

I was trying to chug my cocoa before it froze in my stomach on the way down. I was anxiously waiting for the sun to come up, to give us some relief. I watched the thermometer painstakingly tiptoe upward to a stifling negative fourteen degrees Fahrenheit from negative forty-three. Assuming no one froze to death, we would have survived another night.

Sitting, keeping watch, always made me reflect and wonder how exactly the world had ended up this way, what had really happened. I knew the truth was that nobody knew for sure, but I couldn't help but think about how much our government—or any government—knew about what happened or even what would happen? Struggling to get the image out of my head of a decapitated Joshua, I wondered if First Contact had anything to do with bringing about this frozen hell.

SIX YEARS AGO
(Part One)

President Michael Eastman...

EIGHT

President Michael Eastman was a very handsome man. Some believed even too handsome to truly want to go into politics beyond the PTA of his hometown of Carrboro, North Carolina, a suburb within Chapel Hill. But in spectacular fashion, he rose from PTA to city council to mayor to senator and, lastly, to the highest office in the land.

President Eastman sat at his desk in the Oval Office. A mug of room-temperature tea sat on the table without a coaster, along with a landline telephone—an ancient relic, but still one of the most secure forms of long-distance communication.

That's all.

There were no briefs, no National Security reports, no economic reports, and no laundry list of calls to international leaders that he had to return.

Even though he was entering week twelve of his first term in office, he had aged as though he were in the closing days of his fifth four-year term. He had already forgotten the two other men in the unlit room with him that had entered just a few moments before.

"Mr. President," said Vice President Patrick Sans softly, "did you need anything?"

"No," the President said quickly without making eye contact as he stared at his mug with a child's finger-painted drawing of an eagle. His voice was almost at a whisper and he was exhausted beyond words.

"Shall we come back later?" the second man, General Frank Keats, said. He was dressed in full military garb with several medals hanging from his shirt like a tacky Christmas tree.

"Of course not," Eastman said. "We must do this now."

He stood and looked out the window towards the Rose Garden. All that remained was a huge pile of dirt surrounded by little craters all around.

Further outward, the streets of Washington DC were in total ruin. The same could be said for every other major city in the country. One large military Hummer and some small tanks used the city street as their personal parking lot. The only people on the streets were elite Navy SEALS and Army Rangers armed to the teeth.

"Mr. President?" General Keats was the first to speak after another long pause. His medals quietly jingled like an out-of-tune wind chime as he stepped forward. "I think it's time we consider *all* of our options." He confirmed that his posture was erect as President Eastman turned to face him. General Keats continued, "With all due respect, sir, have you considered *all* the options?"

"Of course, I have, General!" Eastman shouted as Keats tried to stand even straighter, nearly snapping his surgically-fused spine in the process.

"Given the event that occurred twenty-seven days ago, coupled with what our remaining scientists are telling us, we should initiate Operation Periodic East," said the Vice President with slight hesitation.

What the Vice President was referring to that occurred twenty-seven days ago was that an unidentified nation launched a nuclear weapon; one of quite a few that had been fired from several nations. But this particular warhead, whether intended to or not, hit a nuclear stockpile. The immediate result was catastrophic. An incalculable number of people died instantly.

The long-term effects for everyone within the thousand mile radius was a slow and painful death.

"I agree with the Vice President, sir," Keats said.

"I will not give that order, gentlemen," President Eastman replied firmly.

"There's nothing more we can do, Mr. President."

"Did you just tell the leader of the free world what he can or can't do, General?"

"Oh, give it up already, Frank," the Vice President stepped in front of General Keats and slammed his hands on the President's desk.

"I will not give up on my country, Patrick. How dare you? We knew what we were inheriting when we were sworn in again eighty-three days ago.

"The NSA couldn't have even predicted this. None of our agencies or allies' agencies could have predicted this. Public, private, and pirate corporations had no idea. Even the conspiracy theorists, who are apophenic to the core, couldn't conceive of something like this."

The Vice President gripped a folding chair opposite the President's desk in a threatening posture. General Keats took a step toward the Vice President but didn't try to restrain him.

"Enough!" Eastman shouted, causing both men to return to military positions.

"Don't forget I served my country, too, General."

Vice President Patrick Sans was clearly not going to tolerate his surroundings much longer. Particularly that of General Frank Keats still in his line of sight.

"Let's go downstairs," President Eastman said almost in a whisper but his subtext was loud and clear.

They were going to access an underground tunnel in the West Wing that was top secret to everyone except those three men. Not even the other members of the first family knew, but it didn't matter. All the members of the first family had perished four days before in a domestic terrorist attack.

42

NINE

Sam emerged from his shower pruned and still enraged. Three hours and nineteen minutes were not long enough to soak and scrub away his embarrassment or rage.

"SIS, where is Kairi Miyaki?"

The muted clicks amplified slightly.

"Dr. Kairi Miyaki is not on board Icarus," SIS replied.

Confusion flooded Sam's prior demeanor.

"Where is she?"

A few more clicks, but no other response came from SIS. This was very unusual. In the six years that Icarus had been operating, SIS had never malfunctioned even slightly, according to its diagnostic records.

"Where is Captain Bellamy?"

A few clicks.

"Captain Katherine Bellamy is not on board Icarus."

"What?" Sam took a deep breath. "SIS, where is Samuel Ng?"

A few clicks.

"Samuel Ng is in his quarters."

"Okay, at least it knows I'm here," he said aloud to himself. "How many people are on board Icarus right now?"

A few clicks.

"Icarus has a crew of one; Samuel Ng."

Sam rubbed his ears to make sure no water was still inside. He couldn't believe what he just heard.

"SIS, repeat what you just said."

A few clicks.

"Icarus has a crew of one; Samuel Ng."

Sam rubbed his eyes. He had to have been dreaming. Or SIS was malfunctioning. Or both. He quickly got dressed and started down his corridor.

So far, he hadn't seen or heard anyone.

"Hello?" Sam shouted but no response. "Anybody? This isn't funny." Still nothing. "SIS, are you there?"

A few clicks.

"Yes, Samuel Ng."

"How long would it take for you to run a full diagnostic on yourself and Icarus? Check for life signs, ship efficiency, everything."

SIS first responded with several more clicks than usual and louder. "Approximately eighteen minutes."

"Do it and report the results to me once it's complete."

A few clicks again.

"Affirmative."

Sam was running as he turned several sharp corners and stopped at the Mess Hall. Usually a lively place at all hours with at least a dozen crew members at any given time, it was empty with no evidence that anyone had ever been there before.

"What the—Hello!?" Sam yelled at the top of his lungs.

The echo bounced off the walls only to be heard again by Sam himself. Slithering between tables, he made his way into the kitchen; somewhere Sam had never been or even thought about. He walked to the first of a long line of industrial refrigerators and freezers pressed against a wall that seemed the length of a few football fields. He opened the first refrigerator and found it empty. Then, another. He continued this for several minutes. Everything was empty. Not one morsel of food.

"It's gotta be finished by now," Sam said. Sure enough, those familiar clicks started again.

"Diagnostic complete." But SIS didn't say anything else. Sam looked up at the ceiling.

"And?"

A few clicks.

"Please specify your request."

"SIS, where is Kairi Miyaki?"

"Dr. Kairi Miyaki is not on board Icarus."

"Is Samuel Ng the only member on board?"

"Affirmative."

"How is that possible?"

A few clicks.

"Unable to analyze request."

Sam walked out of the kitchen and made his way to the Bridge; another area of the ship that he had never seen as he did not have the necessary rank or authority to enter the Bridge unless personally requested by Captain Bellamy.

The Bridge had a control console at the front of it that was nearly as long as the room itself. One solitary chair was bolted to the floor at the center of the console.

"I guess that's my seat," he said.

Everything looked in working order, but there was no way for Sam to be sure.

"SIS, what is the result of the diagnostic?"

A few clicks.

"Diagnostic complete. Icarus is operating at one hundred percent. No other issues to report."

"What the fuck?"

Suddenly, Sam heard the Bridge door open. He turned and saw someone he'd never seen before enter. The man didn't notice Sam standing on the opposite end of the Bridge until Sam spoke.

"Hello?" Sam said.

The unknown man immediately turned toward Sam and pointed a military-grade weapon at him.

"Hands up," he said with a militaristic tone.

Sam immediately complied.

It was the first time he had ever seen a weapon on Icarus.

TEN

The morning sun didn't fully show. It hid behind nimbostratus clouds, which meant a bad storm was about to hit.

Never mind trying to find Icarus in the sky today, I figured.

Everyone who had left camp with me was alive and accounted for. Ada was still sleeping, but Daniel was feeling surprisingly spry and insisted on helping Miles and I to prepare breakfast.

"I cook. I cook," he kept repeating while he helped Miles start the fire.

Sara was also still sleeping in Miles's tent and we thought it best to just let her be as the other survivors bravely made their way out into the cold open air. As the snow in the pot melted and then painstakingly starting to boil, Miles looked up at the sky. We could see the clouds starting to part. The very point in the sky that parted was where Icarus was visible. Only this time, it was doing something none of us had ever seen before… It was blinking.

Normally, its lights would reflect off the sun and have a translucent and beaming glow, but we had never seen it blink.

"Do you see that, Tiberius?" Miles asked.

"I do see it."

"What do you suppose it means?"

Suddenly, a familiar and terrifying roar was heard in

the distance.

"Trouble. Trouble for all of us."

Polar bears were closing in on our location. Miles and the others had abandoned their breakfast as the winds started to pick up. He went over to his tent and woke Sara.

"We need to start moving now," I heard him say.

Sara had rolled out of her tent and understood what she had to do and packed quickly.

In the midst of all this insanity, I was thinking of home. I missed home. I missed summers. Real summers.

Growing up in the French Quarter, I was a man who, once upon a time, appreciated the arts of the city. It was unlike any other on Earth. And the Earth was finally starting to appreciate that. But it wasn't only the sounds of home that I longed for. It was also the smells; the food. I still remembered the last time I had gumbo from my favorite spot—Mr. B's Bistro on Royal Street. Their signature dish was called the Gumbo Ya Ya. The last time I had some was on April 8th, 2057; nine days before The Blast. I was with Dana, a girl I had been seeing for almost a year and I finally thought I was ready to settle down, as the ancient saying goes. I really thought she was the one.

Dana was a civil engineer born and raised on the bayou. The last sixteen generations of her family had all lived on the same land that was originally colonized by French settlers. She was New Orleans through and through. Why she gave a fourth-generation Romanian kid the time of day was beyond me.

I was planning to propose the next time I saw her. I had even purchased the ring. But I lost contact with Dana after The Blast. I had spoken to her mere hours before, making plans to meet up after we got off work, but then the world changed. Everything went to the seventh circle of hell and beyond.

After The Blast, survivors were sent to SuperDome Hospital. The once professional stadium of an ancient sport called football was converted into a hospital and shelter after professional American football worldwide was banned in 2034.

My father worked nearly ninety hours a week at that hospital as an anesthesiologist, and that was *before* The Blast. My mother was a history professor at Loyola University. Both of them loved their jobs. My sister Claire was studying to be a veterinarian in Scotland at the time, but The Blast killed her instantly. Most of the United Kingdom became a crater in minutes. My mother died about two months later after she was trampled to death during a looting riot. My father died of exhaustion staying awake to treat patients and insisting he didn't need rest after working for eight days straight without sleep and very little food.

After The Blast, I had made my way to the Super-Dome, but I never saw Dana there. I was convinced that she either didn't survive or died soon after.

I came out of my momentary daze of reflection by being side-swiped across the face by blizzard winds.

Miles double-checked that his and Sara's tent was secure and said again, "Tiberius, let's move!"

"Yes," I said, almost still in my daze.

"You okay?"

"Just thinking of home."

"We can't go home," Miles retorted. "We have to survive."

Miles was nothing if not a survivor and a fighter.

Every soldier, reserve officer, law enforcement officer—and really anyone with any kind of medical or search and rescue training worldwide—was tasked to search for survivors when The Blast happened.

The survivors, all of us, knew that we had made it through the other side of what we believed to be the global "reset button" being pressed. But what no one obviously expected was for us to have to overcome this frozen tundra of a place. It was getting old. It was becoming harder and harder to survive. It was becoming harder and harder to maintain any hope or optimism of life returning to any sense of "normal" that once was—a planet that had distinguishable seasons, broadcast television, and gumbo.

We finished packing and started moving. Miles, Sara, and I took the lead while Ada took the rear of the line with the other survivors. We were all tired, cold, but we were always tired and cold. But this relocating felt like something else. I could see it in everyone's faces. It was getting harder and harder to keep the belief that we somehow wouldn't die the way we had been living. That we wouldn't all end up like just another survivor too stubborn not to die right away. But we had to keep moving—or as the saying went—"die trying."

ELEVEN

"*Woah!* Wait! Put that down," Sam pleaded to the stranger pointing the weapon.

"Who are you?" the man asked.

"Sam. Samuel Ng."

The stranger stayed silent, his weapon still drawn.

"You want to tell me who you are?" Sam asked, starting to breathe heavily.

"What am I doing here?" the stranger asked.

"I don't know, pal. You just walked in and started pointing that thing at me. Do you know what'll happen if you fire a weapon here?"

The stranger looked around confirming no one else was on the Bridge and slowly lowered and holstered his weapon. Sam took a deep sigh of relief and slowly lowered his hands.

"Can we start over?" Sam asked.

"What do you do here?" the stranger asked.

"Me?" Sam replied. "I'm just a Liaison. A middleman. A glorified mediator. I fix problems between people."

The man stared silently, attentively listening as if this was the first time he had heard these words spoken in that precise order.

"What do *you* do here?" Sam asked. "How is it that I've never seen you after being on Icarus for nearly eleven years? Icarus is big, but it's not that big."

The man didn't respond. Sam gave an annoyed and

audible sigh.

"SIS, who is on the Bridge with me?"

A few clicks.

"Samuel Ng is the only person on board."

"Well, that's broken," Sam declared. "I didn't think that could happen."

The stranger finally spoke, "But you can fix it, right? You just said—"

"I fix problems between *people*. I don't work with the AI," Sam interjected as he walked slowly over to another control console, checking for other system malfunctions, though he was unable to find any. He continued, "We need Kairi for that."

"Kairi?"

"Dr. Kairi Miyaki, she built SIS, the computer system that handles all of the ship's inner workings. This is probably a huge joke that Kairi is pulling on me for calling her a 'fucking bitch.' It has just occurred to me that you're probably a Holo-program, which explains why I've never seen you on board before and why SIS can't identify you."

"Why would you call her that?"

"Not important. Can you help me find her?"

"Is she dangerous?"

Sam found this question especially odd considering that the stranger had been pointing a weapon at him just two minutes before.

"SIS, show me an image of Kairi Miyaki."

Suddenly, a three-dimensional Holo-program image of Kairi manifested at the center of the Bridge. It looked like a realistic wax copy that people used to make in tacky twentieth-century museums on the west coast of the United States once upon a time.

"Well, at least that works," Sam said.

"She's cute."

"Don't let that fool you," Sam retorted.

"So she *is* dangerous."

Sam was done entertaining his rude guest or intruder or possible Holo-program or whatever he was trying to classify him as. "Can you please cut the act and tell me who you are?"

No response.

"Damn it! SIS, who is on the Bridge with me?"

A few clicks.

"Samuel Ng is in his quarters."

"What?"

Suddenly, Sam was in his quarters, sitting up in bed and soaked in sweat. A lucid dream, maybe. How could it have felt that real? Had he been drugged? He looked at his sleeves to see that he was indeed wearing his sleeping attire. He couldn't remember anything after his three-hour shower.

"SIS, how many people are on board Icarus?"

A few clicks.

"There are seventy-seven people on board Icarus."

"She's working now," Sam said to himself.

"Where is Kairi Miyaki?"

A few clicks.

"Dr. Kairi Miyaki is in the Mess Hall."

Sam decided to get up and pay her another visit.

TWELVE

The Mess Hall was exactly how Sam had seen it every day since Icarus launched; full, vibrant, and loud. An array of people sat with their typical cliques; Sam stood in line and grabbed a tray as he looked at what was on the day's menu.

Peanut butter and banana pancakes; the diarrhea-plugging breakfast of champions. Along with an array of heavily concentrated juices and soy and pork sausages. As he looked around waiting to serve himself, he noticed Kairi sitting alone at her usual table. She didn't have any food with her, of course. Just tea and her digital pad.

Kairi was an enigma of a person. A person with her intellect had to be, but rumors of her sexual proclivities and animalistic prowess were transitioning into confirmed facts. The only thing that outdid her intelligence was her beauty. And she knew it. For her, sex was a form of control and not companionship, passion, or even lust. Her biographer had written that she had been sexually assaulted by a college professor when she was eight years old; a claim that Kairi had vehemently denied. The book also claimed that she was unable to bear children, but Kairi *did* confirm that. Despite her promiscuity, the world needed more intelligent minds like that of Kairi Miyaki.

Sam considered approaching—with caution, of course. He

should have never called her a "fucking bitch." He walked up to her knowing full well the exchange would not make him feel any better. In fact, it would probably make him feel worse, but he knew he had to swallow his pride.

He walked up to her table, still holding his tray. He tried to keep eye contact with her, but his gaze kept wandering as he spoke.

"I want to apologize," he blurted softly.

"For?" she queried, not looking up from her pad.

"For what I said. I was angry."

"Yes, you were," she said followed by a predictable sigh.

"Will you forgive me?" he asked genuinely.

"If that's what you need to get through the day, then yes, I forgive you."

Sam bit his lip to keep himself from starting another winless argument. Kairi finally looked up from her pad and looked Sam square in the eye.

"Anything else?"

"Did you at least enjoy it?"

"The sex?"

"Uh huh," Sam sheepishly responded, regretting his question.

"I've had worse, but I've also had better," she replied with a smile.

"Have a good life, Kairi," Sam said, trying to hide his defeat.

"You too, Sam," Kairi responded, turning her attention back to her digital pad.

Sam walked away still holding his tray uncertain as to what had happened and how many people were paying adequate attention to their exchange. He extended his arm between two people in line getting their food, grabbed a fistful of bacon, and shoved it into his mouth as he plopped his tray down at a table with a group of men he had never spoken to before.

THIRTEEN

Sara was asleep riding piggyback on Miles's back as we worked our way through the Ice Jungle inch by inch. We seemed to have moved away from the polar bears in time as we couldn't hear any anymore. Ada had allowed me to lead the way, but I stopped in my tracks when we came across the mouth of a large cave, one I had never seen before. We had been walking for over four hours, which considering the depth of the snow and the direction and strength of the wind, was just about two miles, but exhaustion was setting in.

I noticed a flickering light from inside the cave, and Miles must have noticed it too because he gingerly lowered Sara down and woke her up. She rubbed her eyes.

"Is that heaven?" she asked in a sleepy voice.

Miles sighed but didn't answer. I looked behind him and noticed less than a handful of the original camp members remained; one of them, of course, was Daniel. Some members had told me in the last day or so that they wouldn't go on with us. They had given up. Unfortunately, it was too dangerous to stay with them or try to convince them to keep moving. One survivor in particular, I saw simply stopped marching, turned around, and buried himself in the snow. We were dropping like flies.

But not Daniel.

It truly was astonishing how Daniel had managed to survive and outlast literally everyone in his home. In his famly. In his town. In his country. Daniel struggled his way to the front and joined Miles and I as we discussed whether or not to venture inside.

On the one hand, it would be a perfect spot to stay the night. On the other, the risk of encountering rogue, solitary survivors was a high possibility, especially since most rogue survivors were severely deformed and infected from The Blast. Additionally, the likelihood of them being dangerous psychologically and/or physically was all but certain.

"*Interesante*," Daniel whispered, more to himself than the rest of us.

"Miles," Sara spoke up but he quickly shushed her.

"If we can stay in there tonight, we won't freeze," I said.

"But we might die," Miles countered.

"But we might die," I repeated in agreement.

Voices sounded from inside the cave and seemed to grow louder. We moved a little closer to the mouth of the cave, trying to see if we could find the cause of the noise.

"Mom! Dad!" Sara shouted, trying to run inside.

I immediately lunged forward and covered her mouth. The indistinct conversation stopped and a loud commotion was heard. Then, the light source quickly faded like a warm mist.

Miles carried his feet over the snow as quickly as he could toward the mouth of the cave. I followed closely behind him leaving Sara with Ada.

The ground quickly changed from shin-deep snow to a ground-level slush. I felt a level of warmth that was now foreign to me, to all of us. So much so that I felt I was actually starting to sweat. Miles unsheathed his machete and went inside.

Upon entering, I found remains of a large fire that had just been put out, but no food, no makeshift cookery, no clothes or pelts, no other signs of inhabitants.

"Hello?" Miles called. "We won't hurt you. Please show yourself."

No sound was heard for a few moments until an unfamiliar sound echoed within the cave.

"*Bakarrik zaude?*"

And then, something terrifying and spectacular happened.

A voice from the other direction replied, "*Ez nago bakarrik.*"

It was Daniel, who, having heard another speak his mother tongue, moved quickly to the head of the group.

FOURTEEN

SIS was in fine working order as far as Sam could tell. Whatever diagnostic hiccup SIS had was non-existent at best, immediately corrected at worse in his mind or just a figment of his imagination.

He had plopped himself and his tray down at a table normally reserved for an intimate clique of workers simply known as *The Gators*. They were five highly specialized hydroelectric engineers who all had one job: make sure all the shit vented into space and only space.

To call them plumbers was an insult beyond all insults in their minds, but that's what they were. The five-man team split shifts to ensure that "the ship never took a shit." That was their motto.

Sam felt compelled to ask, "You guys haven't had any problem with SIS, have you?"

The Gators all looked at each other in silence for a moment unsure of what to make of this uninvited guest at their table.

"No," the oldest of them finally said slowly.

"Not our department at least," the youngest one said.

"I know," Sam interjected. "I was just curious if—"

"Talk to Dr. Miyaki if you have issues with SIS. Or if that doesn't help, check with MAC," the oldest one said.

Sam's eyebrows furled upwards as he asked, "Who's Mac? Where can I find him?"

"MAC is not a who, it's a what. It stands for 'Malfunctions Access Computations.' If SIS had an issue, MAC would tell you," the third Gator spoke. He continued, "It's a failsafe within a failsafe within a failsafe. Like the *Inception* of digital security bureaucracy. Remember that classic?"

"How do I access it?" Sam asked, disregarding the Gator's sudden nostalgia.

"With Dr. Miyaki's authorization. She and Captain Bellamy are the only ones who can access it," the oldest Gator said.

"It's only been used once; right before Icarus launched. It was to quintuple check everything," the youngest Gator added.

"How come I don't remember that?" Sam asked.

"The Gators were the last people onboard to enter hypersleep. Dr. Miyaki was very keen on ensuring that there wouldn't be any shit to clean up when everybody woke up," the youngest Gator said.

"Priorities," the oldest Gator snorted.

Sam sat in silence for a moment, taking it all in. He thanked the Gators for their time and got up with his tray, forgetting to eat. He knew he had to talk to Kairi *again* despite it only being minutes after telling her to have a good life.

FIFTEEN

Daniel shouted again the same phrase as he enthusiastically, but slowly, made his way through the mouth of the cave.

"*Ez nago bakarrik. Zuregana etorriko gara.*"

I was right behind Daniel holding onto his shoulder.

"Daniel, what's going on?" I asked.

"It's good, Tiberius. It's good," Daniel whispered back.

"Do they speak English? Or Dutch? Miles speaks Dutch."

We inched our way to Miles who was still surveying what remained of the campsite. He removed his hat and wiped away the sweat from his forehead and stared at it for a moment as if it were a foreign object.

"Let's keep moving. Daniel can talk to him," I said.

"Him who?" Miles asked.

He raised an excellent point. We had no idea who these people were. They could be dangerous. They probably *were* dangerous. As far as I knew, no one had spoken Basque other than Daniel that survived The Blast.

"It's really warm," I finally admitted.

We all stared at each other in silence as the rest of the tribe we had left outside creeped forward to join us. Once inside and warmth beginning to spread over our mildly frozen bones, the remaining group and I listened attentively for any other kind of response. But no luck. Then, something occurred to me, something terrifying.

What if the responses Daniel was shouting were to the aliens? Hadn't they spoken some type of dialect when we had First Contact?

I looked at Miles and extended my arm to stop him from walking forward. I applied light pressure on Daniel's shoulder and he stopped.

"Daniel," I began. "Who are you talking to? Ask if they are human."

SIXTEEN

Sam saw Kairi surprisingly still sitting in the same spot. Normally, when Kairi was seen on the ship, she never stayed in the same spot for more than a few minutes. Sam looked down at his tray still filled with food and dumped it in the bin as he made his way back to her table.

"I need to ask for a favor," he said.

"Again? I told you I've had worse. Take it as a compliment," she replied, not looking up from her digital pad.

"Your failsafe system, MAC, I need to access it," Sam said, his tone firmer than what he meant it to be.

"If you have an issue with SIS, every person on board has access to—"

"This isn't a diagnostic or troubleshooting issue," Sam interrupted. "Give me a little more—"

"Credit?" Kairi interjected. "You're a Liaison. Can you even tie your shoes?"

"Yes," Sam said, annoyed. "Kairi, come on, you and I just had—"

"Sex? Yes. And you gave me an orgasm. Bravo. You're as useful to me as a rubber tube," she continued.

"Oh my God, you *bitch*, listen to me!" Sam shouted much louder than he should have.

The Mess Hall was stone silent. Kairi raised an eyebrow as she took a sip of her tea.

"Now that you have everyone's attention," she started.

"What is so important and complicated that you need access to my personal diagnostic system? The diagnostic system that's meant for running, you know, things like quadruple life support backup checks. What is your issue that is so grave that you need MAC?"

"I need to run a MAC scrub on SIS itself and the ship," Sam said lowly.

Silence filled the air as Kairi did a loud exhale and stood from her seat.

Then, she replied with a simple and sharp, "No."

"What do you mean 'No?'"

"MAC cannot run a scrub on the whole ship right now. That takes thirty hours and all the crew would have to be put in hypersleep because life support would temporarily shut down. The Captain would never approve that."

"Sounds like a flaw in your design," Sam countered.

With that response, Kairi seemed to show her first public human response ever: anger.

"SIS can run its own scrub on Icarus at any time without compromising life support in eighteen to twenty-two minutes."

"That's only a preliminary diagnostic and you know that," Sam argued.

Kairi stares back hard at Sam before saying, "Fine, let's speak to the Captain."

"Now?"

"Why not?" she fired back. "This is clearly an emergency, right? Even if I wanted to run a MAC scrub, I still need her approval. I'll do it, but you have to convince her, and then maybe, just maybe, I can run a MAC scrub."

Sam gave a nervous smile, still feeling all the eyes of the Mess Hall weighing on him. Kairi refilled her tea and gestured her arm outward towards the exit.

"After you," she said.

SEVENTEEN

Deeper and deeper, we went into the cave, which seemed to have no end in sight. We were feeling actual, natural warmth. That should've been my first clue that something was not normal.

However, Daniel pressed on desperately.

Imagine not being able to speak to anyone in your own mother language because they had all presumably died out, and then began hearing it again after countless years.

But we still hadn't seen anyone or anything.

"Daniel, what have you been saying?" I asked.

But all Daniel could say in response was what he kept repeating. "It's good, Tiberius. It's good."

He began to try to run and I tried my best to get him to slow down, but he wouldn't listen or didn't understand.

"We're getting pretty deep into the cave," Miles whispered. "What if we have to run? Daniel... The kids... Sara can't—"

"You're right," I said, cutting Miles off. "We should head back and come up with a plan in case we run into someone or something. Or if it's a trap," I said, speaking loudly so everyone could hear me.

Then, suddenly, amazingly, incredibly, we found something that none of us had ever seen before.

EIGHTEEN

Captain Katherine Bellamy stood in her spacious, but sparsely decorated Captain's quarters—not to be confused with her personal quarters. There were some framed family photos on her desk of her husband, children, and one grandchild; all killed, as far as she knew, in The Blast.

She was staring out the window, facing the heavens, contemplating—as she often did—while sipping a hot chocolate. A muted chime interrupted her trance-like thoughts as she turned towards her door.

"Come in," her soothing but commanding voice replied.

Katherine Bellamy was an Army brat through and through. She then became the mother of Army brats. Both her parents, her four grandparents, as well as her great-grandparents all served. Katherine lived all over the world, and on her eighteenth birthday, she enlisted and never looked back. She was the first woman in United States history to achieve the rank of Five-star General. Soon after, she received unanimous nominations and votes to be named Captain of Icarus. She didn't even have to campaign.

Kairi and Sam walked in together and saluted her.

"Captain, good morning," Sam began. Kairi just sat down immediately without being offered to sit.

"Good morning, you two," she began as she sat and motioned for Sam to sit as well. "To what do I owe the pleasure?”

"He wants to run a MAC scrub on SIS, which would result in Icarus being completely shut down," Kairi blurted out unceremoniously. No pleasantries. No small talk.

"I see," Captain Bellamy replied while sipping her hot chocolate. "Why?"

Sam suddenly felt a rush of nerves course through him. He felt as if he could run a marathon full sprint and shit his pants all at the same time. He remembered his encounter with the unidentified man who pointed a weapon at him on the Bridge.

He remembered how he was suddenly in his quarters in his sleeping attire soaked in sweat. He cleared his throat and stammered before he was finally able to get out his first cohesive sentence.

"I think I'm losing my mind."

An expression of genuine shock entered both women's faces.

"Well," Captain Bellamy began, "we certainly can't have that."

"I'm sorry, Captain," Sam said. "I remember… I remember getting out of the shower this morning, asking SIS where Kairi was located, and SIS responded saying that I was the only person on board. I entered the Mess Hall and it was entirely empty. Not just of people, but of food, supplies, everything. I entered the Bridge and it was empty. Then, I saw a man; someone I had never seen before. He had a weapon pointed at me."

Kairi and Captain Bellamy remained silent as Sam continued.

He started speaking faster at this point. "Even though I convinced him to put his weapon down, he wouldn't tell me who he was, what his role was on Icarus, or why he was even in the Bridge in the first place. Then, before I knew it, I was back in my quarters, soaking wet. And everything was—"

"Back to normal?" Captain Bellamy asked.

"Yes, ma'am," Sam replied sheepishly.

Captain Bellamy took another sip of her hot chocolate as she looked at both Sam and Kairi. Sam looked embarrassed beyond saving while Kairi continued to look annoyed.

"Dr. Miyaki, what do you think?" Captain Bellamy asked.

"About what, Captain?"

"Do you think Sam has expressed adequate reasoning for running a MAC scrub on SIS?"

"No," Kairi said bluntly. "He just had a bad dream."

"What about this unrecognizable person you spoke of?" Captain Bellamy asked. "Could you describe him to see if anyone recognizes him? It may have been just a malfunction of a Holo-program one of the other members of the crew had been running. It is rare, but glitches in the Holo-program have happened from time to time."

Sam remained silent as Captain Bellamy leaned forward in her chair.

"Sam, have you ever had any experiences like this before? Lucid dreams, sleepwalking? Do you take any medication or use any alternative means to help you sleep?"

"No, Captain."

"Was there anything different last night about how or when you went to sleep? You know, something different in your routine," Captain Bellamy pried.

Sam naturally thought of the fact that he had slept with Kairi last night. He wasn't sure if he could or was required to answer that kind of personal question. Before he could stammer through another response, Kairi spoke for him.

"We spent the night together last night in my quarters," Kairi said, almost a hint of boredom in her tone.

Captain Bellamy looked at Kairi with a truly disappointed expression that even surprised Kairi. Captain Bellamy stood and walked toward her window again looking out at Earth on the horizon.

"Thank you, Mr. Ng. That will be all. I cannot grant your request of running a MAC scrub on SIS at this time. You haven't proven to me that it is worth taking up that much time and risk."

"I understand, Captain. Thank you for your time," Sam said as he rose and saluted her.

Kairi got up to do the same and was about to walk out when Captain Bellamy spoke.

"Dr. Miyaki, if you could please stay a moment," Captain Bellamy requested.

Kairi sat back down as Sam quietly walked out of the Captain's quarters. After Sam walked out, Captain Bellamy sat back down.

"Kairi, I'm not going to sit here and try to outsmart you, outwit you, or do anything of the sort that would make you feel inferior or intimidated. We both know that you're too smart for that and intimidation is not really my style," she began while Kairi remained silent. "Lucky for me, I'm the Captain, and that means I don't have to resort to intimidation anyways. All I have to do is order something from a crew member and they do it. It's actually a really neat trick. "

"Why are you telling me this, Captain?"

"I normally do not get into the personal affairs of any of the lives of my crew unless it affects their work. I know that you've been spreading your legs the length of this ship since soon after we left home. It hasn't affected your work, but it has affected the work of some others. I don't know what you do or say to them, but you cannot let this continue."

"Captain, you say that you don't get into others' personal affairs, but yet you tell me to not spend time with other members of the crew?"

"I'm telling you that if you want to get laid, create a Holo-program for it from now on. Not even you would be able to tell the difference. Stop screwing with the minds and hearts of the people on board and try screwing one of your toys," Captain Bellamy proclaimed, taking a final swig of her hot chocolate before continuing.

"I remember the questions you asked most of the male candidates during their final interview. I thought those questions were meant to throw them off and to see how well they respond to random and unexpected challenges, but you actually tried to turn a process that our lives depended on into your personal dating game."

Dr. Kairi Miyaki rose from her seat; something that should never be done while the Captain is still seated unless dismissed. Captain Bellamy glared at her as she stood and adjusted her uniform.

"'Stop screwing with the minds and hearts of the people on board and screw one of my toys.' Is that an order, Captain?" Kairi retorted confrontationally, getting a little too close to Captain Bellamy's personal space for her liking.

"Dismissed," Captain Bellamy snarled.

Kairi kept her gaze and expression for a few more seconds, then smiled and walked out.

SIX
YEARS
AGO
(Part Two)

First Contact...

NINETEEN

The "downstairs" that President Eastman had been referring to was a staircase located in the War Room of the White House. The War Room was the room that had been used for centuries as the location where wars were started and avoided; won and lost. Inside was only one analyst in a room usually occupied by dozens of the most experienced military strategists on the planet. All you needed to get in was a key card and Eastman, Sans, and Keats each had their own.

General Frank Keats swiped his card and the door clicked open. He held the door for President Michael Eastman and Vice President Patrick Sans. The lone analyst, a young man named Simon, stood as was the custom. President Eastman immediately motioned for him to sit.

"Thank you, Simon. Please, have a seat," he said soothingly.

Simon sat and continued working his console. General Keats approached him, standing over his shoulder.

"What have you found?" Keats asked.

"Nothing good," Simon responded, continuing to work his console and not looking back. "Chatter is… complicated. Some are making peace with certain deities while others are making threats that can be ignored because their claims are clearly impossible at this point."

"What sort of threats?" Vice President Sans asked.

"Well, one woman is live streaming, claiming to be the

new Queen of Finland and has made demands for millions of Euros and claims to have a hostage," Simon said.

"Explain to me why that's not a viable threat," Sans demanded.

"Because Finland doesn't exist anymore," General Keats answered.

"Because the Euro lost all its value twenty-seven days ago," President Eastman said.

"And because the woman's hostage is confirmed to be a doll. She's also broadcasting from a canoe in the middle of the Indian Ocean," Simon added, zooming out of the satellite drone image.

The Vice President stood in stunned silence and was cut off before he would try to speak again.

"Simon," President Eastman began, "I want to thank you for—"

Suddenly, a low hum buzzed from Simon's console. He closed the woman's broadcast and put on his headset, frantically turning knobs and pushing buttons.

"What is it?" General Keats asked.

Simon continued to push buttons before saying, "It's a new signal."

"Origin?" Keats inquired.

"I'm still working that out, but—" Simon stopped himself, almost lost in his turbulent knob turning.

"But what?" Vice President Sans impatiently shouted.

"This is a foreign signal; not out of country foreign. Out of… planet foreign, way past Icarus' location," Simon exhaled.

"Would you explain to me what you're saying in plain English, son?" Vice President Sans asked.

"I think it's alien," Simon replied as General Keats sat in the chair next to him, picked up another headset and quickly found the signal that Simon was listening to.

"My God in Heaven," General Keats said as he began to hear the same sounds that Simon was listening to.

"Fill me in, gentlemen," President Eastman said as General Keats quickly stood and offered Eastman his headset and seat.

"Allow me, sir," Simon said as he pushed another button and pulled the headset from the console.

The sounds coming from the interstellar signal reverberated through the War Room. Shock, fear, excitement, and confusion swirled through every fiber of each man's being.

"Is that—" President Eastman began.

"I think it is, sir," Simon answered. "Communication from space, from another world."

Silence filled the room as each man listened attentively to what was being said. The echo surrounding the room didn't help any until the Vice President finally spoke.

"I know that language," he said slowly.

"What did you just say?" President Eastman asked.

"What do you mean you 'know' that language?" General Keats scoffed. "That's—that's not a 'language.' That's gibberish; it's code. Probably from militias or nut jobs claiming sovereignty somewhere. Our satellites have been repositioned so much. How can you be sure of the origin of that signal?"

"Simon," President Eastman began calmly, "can you tell me the exact origin of that sound?"

Simon looked at his console and typed into his keyboard. An interstellar map was displayed on a screen that took up an entire wall about the size of an IMAX screen.

The Solar System was dead center on the screen, all the planets in their respective places were followed by a fury of other large dots graphed incomprehensibly to nearly everyone in the room except Simon.

"Radio waves are just light waves at a different frequency, Mr. President," Simon began. "When a radio wave is received, the light wave goes on forever at the speed of light. In terms of distance, the strength of the signal in any given direction decreases by a factor of one divided by distance traveled squared because the light spreads. So—"

"So now is the part where you tell us where this is coming from," General Keats said impatiently.

"Further from any signal that can be received by any man-made object on Earth. By far. And when I say 'far,' I'm talking… hundreds of thousands of light years away. But the signal strength is increasing at an incredible rate," Simon continued.

"Thank you, Simon," President Eastman said and then looked over at his Vice President for some answers. "You say you know this language. From where?"

Vice President Sans closed his eyes trying to recall his stellar career of military service and politics. All the amazing and horrific people he had encountered in his fifty-eight years of life. When he finally remembered where he had heard the language before, he nearly kicked himself.

"My wife's grandmother," Sans said suddenly.

"Come again, Patrick?" President Eastman asked, confusion written all over his face.

"My wife's grandmother. She was from a remote village in Northern Spain and she only spoke this language called Basque. She died forty years ago, and with her, most of the people that spoke it. It had been considered a dying language as early as the mid-twentieth century."

"I heard Spain in all that dribble," General Keats began. "They speak Spanish in Spain. Your wife's grandmother was out of her mind."

"General," President Eastman called.

"Sir?" General Keats responded.

"Please tell me that one of the most decorated officers

ever in the United States military who has been around the world at least twenty times is not that naïve."

General Keats stayed silent, unsure of how to respond. There was silence in the room until the most unlikely person spoke.

"Spain has five native languages," Simon blurted.

General Keats looked over at him with an aggravated expression.

"What did you just say, son?" General Keats asked.

"Five languages," Simon began. "Galician-Portuguese, Catalan, Occitan, Basque, and Castilian—what you would probably derive as 'Spanish,' sir. But, I have to agree with Vice President Sans. That signal sounds like Basque."

The three men looked at Simon in shock.

"I audited enough credits to earn myself a Masters in linguistics while working on my Doctorate," Simon said sheepishly, followed by, "I was bored."

"Why aren't you on Icarus?" Keats asked.

"I like to think that I am in a way," Simon responded sheepishly.

President Eastman chuckled a little; a genuine chuckle. He moved closer to Simon's console and then looked up at the screen again.

"Do you know what they're saying?" President Eastman asked.

"I'm sorry, sir. I don't know what they're saying, but I know for sure that that's what is being spoken," Simon declared.

"One hundred percent?" General Keats challenged.

"One hundred percent," Simon snapped back.

He raised the volume on the audio frequency as the four men stood in silence listening without really realizing at that moment that it was to be the single greatest discovery in human history.

TWENTY

I couldn't believe what I was seeing. Daniel had finally stopped after we all reached a vast, wide opening in the cave. It stretched further than I could see. I was starting to wonder how a cave like this formed and how long it took.

It appeared as if a city had been erected. Buildings made of wood, clay, ice, or a combination of the three surrounded us. Some stood up to three stories tall and that didn't even reach half the distance to the top of the cave. In all this splendor, Miles, Sara, Ada, and the rest of us were speechless. But Daniel, Daniel kept shouting in his native Basque. But we didn't see anybody else. The replies had stopped.

"Daniel," Miles began, "What are you saying? What was being said? *¿Comprende*? Who were you talking to?"

Then, a loud shrill came out of Sara that startled all of us. She pointed to… something in the distance walking towards us. Miles had gotten into his military stance and was about to step forward, but Daniel reached for Miles's shoulder and stepped in front of him.

What approached us appeared to be human in the distance, but as it came closer, we knew it wasn't. It was wearing clothes, though not as many layers as we were. Rags, really. As it got closer, I noticed its feet had one toe that stretched out a little further than the rest in the middle of the foot; exactly like the footprint we had found.

Oh, fuck. Was this what killed Joshua? I thought.

It hadn't spoken, but as it got closer, Daniel stepped forward in a display of incredible bravery—some would say borderline psychopathy—and spoke again in his native tongue.

"*Nor zara?*" Daniel asked.

"What are you saying, Daniel?" I asked.

"I ask who he is," Daniel replied.

Sara was trying to disappear behind Miles's legs as the creature stood less than twenty feet away from us. It had a golden hue to its skin and was nearly eight feet tall with a wingspan that likely went beyond that. Its build looked almost exactly human with a few exceptions, as far as I could tell. It had long, slender legs and its feet were identical to the prints I had found a few days ago.

The nearly-larger-than-life-humanoid-creature stayed silent for a moment as it stared us all down. Who knew what it was thinking? Then, it replied in the Basque language. Not by opening its mouth, but by some other means that I couldn't understand. Telepathically? Maybe. It was more as if we were being spoken to by a nearly eight-foot-tall ventriloquist. Its "voice" sounded masculine, but also sounded very… monotone. I didn't know enough about the Basque language to know if inflection was prevalent or if *their* language just sounded like Basque.

Then, most of the group passed out from what I assumed was a combination of shock and unaccustomed heat. Daniel, Miles, Sara, and I were the only ones that hadn't, but the warmth inside the cave was starting to get to me, too.

After about two minutes straight of it *talking*, it stared at Daniel almost as if it knew it would be the only one that can properly communicate with it.

"What did it say, Daniel?" Miles asked.

Daniel was visually frustrated knowing how important it was for him to translate what it said correctly. He looked around the interior of a cave that was nearly the size of a New

York City block, momentarily lost in its grandeur, before he was able to focus again on Miles's question.

"He say…," Daniel began. "He say he visit."

"Visit?" I repeated. "Like *visiting* or a *visitor*? Is he going to leave? Why is he here?"

My questions were piling on and I was speaking way faster than Daniel would be able to keep up. I quickly realized it wasn't a good idea to agitate the only person I knew on the planet that could communicate with this being. I did the best I could by taking a deep breath and starting over.

"Is this the only one of these here? Is he the only one of his kind?" I asked. "Can you ask it that?"

Daniel looked at the being who still hadn't moved and was still staring at Daniel almost with a desperate expression on its face.

"*Bakarrik zaude*?"

"*No*," the creature replied. We all understood that.

"He is not alone," Daniel said ominously.

"How many others?" Miles asked.

"*Zure motako zenbat daude*?"

"*Askoz gehiago.*"

"Many more," Daniel translated.

"Here? Are they all here? In this cave?" Ada asked.

"*Kobazuloan al daude*?"

"*Hainbat lekutan.*"

"Different places," Daniel translated.

I could see that Daniel was getting tired, sweat droplets falling from his face. I stepped forward and said, "We need to rest. He," as I pointed to Daniel, "needs to rest. Where can he rest? Rest, do you understand?"

The creature just stared back with the same non-expression. People in our group who had passed out were coming to and those who had been trembling were gathering the strength to stand. The alien looked behind itself, turned, and started walking. Almost as if a duck had broken ankles, it moved with difficulty. Still, I noticed power in its strides.

Just as I was about to ask about Joshua, its "voice" echoed and reverberated within the massive cave.

"*Jarraitu*."

I looked to Daniel one last time for his help. He smiled weakly.

"We go with him, *Comandante*. It's good, it's good."

TWENTY-ONE

As the Liaison on Icarus, Samuel Ng's duties had become needed more often, but the reasons for his services had become more trivial. Domestic disputes were obviously almost dead in the understood sense of being primarily between spouses. When Icarus first launched, he acted like a bonafide therapist. He helped nearly every crew member, including Captain Bellamy, with issues such as survival remorse, separation anxiety, and feelings of isolation. No matter how big a space—or space itself—felt, and no matter how much free time you had to do anything you wanted, alone was still alone.

Sam was used as a glorified preschool teacher for adults. He had to moderate scheduling disputes for the Holo-program and talk to parents who had no idea how lucky they had it that they had children and were literally helping repopulate the human race, which was one of the primary reasons for Icarus being launched in the first place.

His sessions were by appointment only, but no one paid attention to such a rule anymore. Everyone knew they could just walk in at any time.

✦

As he sat in his office, rereading one of the books he brought from his quarters, Sam heard a muted chime alert him someone was outside wanting to talk to him. He pushed a button on his desk.

"Yes?" Sam replied, "What can I do for you?" But there was no response at first. He pushed the button again. "Come on in," he said as he pushed another button opening the door to his office.

Inside walked a man that looked extremely familiar but was also a man that he had never seen before on Icarus. Except on the Bridge. A few nights before. During his supposed night terror that he still hadn't been able to completely make sense of.

The man sat in a chair across from Sam as he watched the stranger in complete silence.

"You?!" Sam finally said.

"Me?"

"Who are you?"

The man appeared a little upset. "Is this how you treat all your patients when they come to see you for the first time?"

"I'm not a doctor; I don't have patients. I have clients," Sam retorted.

"That's kinda splitting hairs, right?"

Sam took a deep breath and shut his eyes for a moment. When he opened them, the man was still sitting there, shifting uncomfortably in the chair, looking around the office. Sam half-expected him to be gone.

"You're not a Holo-program," Sam said.

The man chuckled and pinched his own arm. "Nope," he began. "I'm very real."

Sam sighed and leaned back in his chair. He tried to remember the little introduction he would say when he first started seeing clients nearly six years ago.

"Welcome," Sam began. "My name is—"

"Sam Ng. Yeah, I know," the man interrupted.

"I don't believe you and I have ever met. What is your name? What do you do here on Icarus?"

"My name is… Jack," he finally managed to get out.

Jack extended his arm across the table to shake Sam's hand and Sam reciprocated. He immediately noticed that Jack's hands were ice cold but didn't bring attention to it.

"Hi, Jack. Nice to officially meet you," Sam said, hiding his grimace to Jack's icy grip.

"Nice to meet you," Jack said back blandly.

The two men sat in another episode of prolonged silence. Jack was a man who appeared to be about Sam's age. He had on dark worker pants and a shirt with what appeared to be a bright yellow stain on it; maybe a sauce of some kind.

"Do you remember what happened on the Bridge a few nights ago?" Sam asked, but Jack only stared back with a silent confused expression. "Nevermind, what can I do for you?" Sam asked.

"I'm lost," Jack said blankly.

"You feel lost?"

"No, I *am* lost," Jack reiterated, "I don't know where I am or how I got here. Or how long I've been here."

Sam was familiar with this. In fact, this was something else that Sam had dealt with himself and helped most people on board Icarus with; the feeling of "loss" was interpreted and experienced differently depending on the person.

In some cases, it was experienced as a loss of identity. For others, a loss of purpose, and in some extreme cases, a loss of being able to distinguish reality from not. Sam figured that Jack was experiencing the latter, though he wondered how it was possible that he had never so much as seen a file for him. He was supposed to have files for everyone on board, whether they ever met with him professionally or not.

Remembering this, he waved his fingers over a translucent screen levitating on his desk. He typed in Jack's name and then looked at him.

"Jack, what is your last name?" Sam asked.

"It's—I don't know."

Sam started to debate with himself over what the proper response was to this question. Ask SIS, of course.

"SIS, who is in my office with me?"

"Samuel Ng is alone in his office," SIS chirped.

"Not again," Sam said. "You're real, right? I'm not dreaming this time, hallucinating, going crazy?"

Jack simply stared back, an unplaceable expression on his face.

"I'm here, Sam," Jack said. Only this time, instead of hearing the monotone, neutrally accented voice that he had been listening to for the last few minutes and had supposedly heard on the Bridge in his night terror or whatever that was, Jack's voice was one of slight cajun drawl. In fact, it was identical to that of his fraternal twin brother; a man named Simon Ng.

SIX
YEARS
AGO
(Part Three)

Initiating Operation Periodic East...

TWENTY-TWO

"*Come* with us, Simon," President Eastman ordered as he walked towards a corner of the War Room with Sans and Keats behind him.

Simon followed closely to where there was no furniture, no painting or map on the wall. Nothing.

"My kids used to play hide and seek in here," President Eastman began. "The Joint Chiefs would get furious with me over it, though they all knew better than to publicly say anything. I didn't care at first until I remembered why they objected to them being here in this particular spot. It wasn't because they were concerned about them being exposed to information sensitive to our national security or risk leaking out classified information. They were just worried about the kids finding the false wall."

President Eastman put his hand flat against a specific spot on the wall and, out of nowhere, a glowing console appeared with a low hum. His palm print suddenly appeared on a digital scan and the wall pushed back and swung open, leaving Simon with a shocked look on his face.

"Not that they'd be able to open it without cutting my hand off first," President Eastman said with a grim smile, remembering his children, when they were still alive, as the men walked down a cavernous hallway through the newly appeared door. "You can shoot this wall with a grenade launcher point blank and it wouldn't even scuff the paint."

Simon followed the three other men down a hallway that expanded surprisingly wide. He went to feel the wall and could sense before touching it that it was humid and even noticed a few branches of ivy growing on it.

"Where are we?" Simon asked. "Am I even allowed to ask, Mr. President?"

"We're in a place that doesn't exist," General Keats said.

"Understood," Simon replied and stayed silent for the remaining agonizing minutes of walking before reaching another door.

President Eastman took a deep breath and turned to Simon. "What you are about to see has never been seen by anyone in my Office, or the Office of any other president for quite some time. It was built in 1938 under FDR's supervision, anticipating the worst from World War II, and had been sealed and opened once more to update its capabilities; on September 12, 2001, by President Cheney."

"You mean Vice President," Simon said, "George W. Bush was President during 9/11."

The Vice President looked back at Simon. "Is that what the history books still say?"

"Through this door," President Eastman started, "I can trigger a chain reaction of sorts that will result in every developed country to go through what is known as 'Periodic East.' All electrical, radio, sonar, and chemical signals will be severed. All the nuclear weapons everyone on the planet has would be converted into paperweights. Think of it like this, if an electromagnetic pulse were an earthquake that spanned the whole planet, it would be the equivalent to stronger than a 500.0 on the scale."

"When the sun rises tomorrow, it will rise in the technological age of Adam and Eve," Vice President Sans said cryptically, "and there's no going back."

"I don't understand," Simon began. "If you do that, you'll stop our soldiers from communicating, sever ties with loved ones who are far apart, and transport of food and resources will come to a grinding halt. You're essentially accelerating the process of worldwide extinction."

"Exactly," General Keats said. "The people of this country—of this world—deserve a merciful death. This is as merciful as we can make it."

"By slowly starving everyone?" Simon argued.

"By killing all hope that mankind has a chance to come out of this in one piece. If you kill hope first, people will die faster, and therefore suffer less," Vice President Sans said.

Simon looked at Sans and Keats, who both had looks of unified determination on their faces. President Eastman was much more docile. Simon could tell that the President wasn't fully on board with this plan.

"Mr. President," Simon pleaded, "if you do this, human history will remember you as the greatest coward who ever lived."

"That's just it," Vice President Sans began.

"After this, there won't be a human history, Simon," President Eastman said as he opened the door.

TWENTY-THREE

Daniel, Miles, and the rest of us were being guided by the alien creature, its voice reverberating off the walls of buildings. Miles and I couldn't stop staring at its feet that seemed to match the imprint we had both seen in the snow a few days before. Miles approached me and spoke softly.

"We need to have Daniel ask it flat out if it killed Joshua," Miles said.

"Not yet," I replied. "I don't know for sure if Daniel would be able to translate that exactly. Besides, do you want to be the first to test how it responds to that kind of accusation?"

Miles remained silent for a moment. We didn't know what to do. We knew that we had mountains of questions, but we didn't know how to ask them—a new kind of communication barrier.

I could see Sara also staring at its feet. Her hesitation and fear seemed to be quickly diminishing and were developing into a full-fledged curiosity. Within nearly a minute, she broke formation and rushed in front of the creature, causing it to stop in its tracks. Miles quickly ran after her, instinctively pulled Sara close, and pushed her behind him. He made no other sudden movements.

The alien creature looked on with an almost child-like curiosity, similar to that of Sara's. It bobbed its head slightly between Sara and Miles and slowly raised its arm to feel the differences in the texture of Mile's and Sara's hair. Then, it put its finger and arm down slowly and continued walking, moving around the siblings.

"How tall are you?" Sara suddenly asked from behind Miles. "Daniel, can you ask him how tall he is? Or what his name is?"

Its name. That would certainly be a start, I thought. I could see that Miles had not been surprised by Sara's questioning. In a way, I wasn't either. We all knew her to be brave, still I imagined Miles was bearing concern as much as I was.

"*Zein da zure izena*?" Daniel asked. I assumed Daniel had asked the latter question and was inquiring about its name.

"*Nire izena da...*," it began, its voice echoing the walls of the cave and of the structures within. But no other sound followed as Daniel looked at it quizzically. Daniel repeated the same words and after a moment the alien responded, "*Ez dakit... Ahaztu egin zait.*"

"He does not know," Daniel said.

"He doesn't know his own name?" Miles repeated.

Daniel simply said, "He forget."

We continued following the alien creature without exchanging any more words. Sara stared at it with a whimsical wonder, her neck straining as she stood inches away from it trying to look up at his face. I couldn't believe how resilient and adaptable she was.

Then, the alien stopped at what seemed to be the center of the cave. There was a building that appeared to be the tallest one out of all of them—there had to have been at least forty buildings. The structure seemed to have been made from banana leaves, bamboo, and other types of fauna from the nearby jungle. There was makeshift furniture that was very large— probably for the alien itself. Miles, who stood over six feet, looked like a child sitting in one of the chairs.

Daniel was pointed to a chair that looked like a throne, complete with extra banana leaf padding on the back. Clearly, the alien immediately saw his importance. The temperature inside the cave was also amazingly warm and getting warmer, warmer than anything we had experienced in years. I looked at my thermometer and it read eighteen degrees Celsius—about sixty-four Fahrenheit. We all slowly started peeling off layers and the alien stared at us in wonder as we did.

Finally, close enough to it, I could see its head was more cylindrical than round. Its skin was the color of cloudy ash and its eyes were jet black without any other shade or pigment. Its nose protruded like an arrowhead from the middle of its face with pulsating nostrils and its ears were small and positioned high on its head near its temple.

I was still very apprehensive, though I did what I could to not show it. Still, I did not know what the alien could *sense* or not. With a front-row view of its features, it seemed that his feet matched nearly exactly like the print I found in the snow next to Joshua's body. If this alien did kill him, then why? Was it defending itself? Was it for food? I had to know.

I couldn't allow myself or the other survivors to get too comfortable, even though that's exactly what we were all feeling. I turned to Daniel who was already starting to doze off.

"Daniel," I began. "Wake up, Daniel."

He looked up at me with exhausted eyes, "Hello, Tiberius," he said.

"Daniel," I said, "I need you to ask the alien something very important, just one more question."

"What question, Tiberius?" he asked, tiredly.

"I need you to ask the alien if it killed Joshua."

Daniel looked at me strangely. I don't think it was because he didn't understand the question, but rather that asking it might offend the creature, and we didn't know what would happen if we were to offend it. It could have dire consequences, but I would have rather known than for us to be killed in our sleep, or worse.

"Please ask it," I said again softly.

Daniel sighed and looked at the alien. He began to stand and it immediately got the alien's attention as it rushed over to help Daniel up. *Not the behavior of a cold-blooded—or whatever-blooded—killer,* I thought.

Daniel immediately went on a ranting spew of his native tongue far more complicated and rapid than I could ever hope to break down. I didn't know if it was supposed to be a precursor before the actual question, or who knows? Finally, Daniel finished saying whatever he said. The alien looked at Daniel and then directly at me. It kept its gaze on me and started walking towards me. Miles immediately stepped in front and was about to unsheathe his machete, but I stopped him.

"Wait," I whispered to Miles.

The alien's voice echoed again throughout the cave with a very short statement.

"*Ez dut hiltzen.*"

I looked over at Daniel who was already gingerly working his way back onto the banana leaf throne. When he was able to arrange himself comfortably again, he looked up at me and said, "He no kill Joshua."

Then, suddenly, the voice echoed again and it surprised even Daniel. I looked to him for another translation. His eyes widened.

"What did he say, Daniel?" I asked, but Daniel remained silent and the alien said it again.

"*Ez dut hiltzen, gure buruzagiak egiten du.*"

As it repeated its response, Daniel's eyes darted between mine and the alien. They were focused, particularly on the creature.

"I no kill," Daniel translated, "but… leader kills."

TWENTY-FOUR

"What did you just say?" Sam asked, his face beginning to sweat and his hands beginning to tremble.

"I said, 'I'm here, Sam,'" Jack began. "I have spent so much time trying to get to you," he continued.

Sam was convinced that he was having a manic episode. He looked around his office to find anything out of place, anything that would confirm his suspicion that he was dreaming, hallucinating, or *dead*. Jack watched Sam as he was beginning to hyperventilate and quickly rose to his aid.

With a gasping breath, Sam said, "Don't touch me. Don't come near me."

Jack's eyes went wide. "Sam," he began.

"Shut up! SIS, who is in my office?"

SIS's familiar muted clicks preempted its response.

"Samuel Ng is alone in his office," it said.

"You're not Simon," Sam started as he was wheezing for a normal breath. "Simon died over six years ago. He... he—" and then Sam vomited all over his desk before passing out.

Sometime later, Sam awoke in his quarters. There was a glass of water on a floating shelf—really a slab of plastic—that was mounted on his wall. He looked around with blurred vision and a pounding headache; his room seemed to be empty. Suddenly, he heard water running from his bathroom sink for a moment, and then, it turned off. Sam sat up in his bed and waited for whomever—or whatever—was in there to come out.

Seconds later, Jack came out with a small towel, drying his hands. He quickly put the towel down and rushed to Sam's side when he saw that he was awake.

"Get away from me," Sam warned. "Who are you? How did you get on board Icarus? Who sent you?" The barrage of questions continued as Sam started hyperventilating again.

Jack quickly gave Sam the glass of water and stepped back as Sam drank. "I'll explain everything that I can remember," Jack began. "I know it's a lot to take in. I'm still not completely clear about what's happened over the last several weeks."

"Weeks? You've been on board for only weeks? How? Earth didn't send up another ship of survivors, did they? Of course they didn't, there's nothing left on Earth to launch a rocket," Sam rationalized out loud.

"I've only been on board for a few days," Jack began, "at least I think it's only been a few days."

"SIS," Sam called, "who is in my quarters?"

"Samuel Ng is alone in his quarters," SIS answered.

This prompted Sam to scream manically. Jack quickly covered Sam's mouth so no one would hear him.

"I might be able to explain why your computer can't 'see' me," Jack began, his hands still pressed to Sam's mouth. "Before this thing went up, everyone had to give some kind of digital and biological footprint to be identified, right? Or a retinal scan or something? Well, I never did that. So, if I never gave the system a way for it to 'see' me, then naturally, it wouldn't be able to."

Sam pondered what Jack had said. Honestly, it made some sense. When the survivors were finalized and confirmed,

Kairi took fingerprints and retinal scans from every member on board and the four that had been born. Without that information, Sam convinced himself at that moment that it would've been possible for SIS to treat Jack as a "ghost" of sorts.

"Sam, I don't know how I got here," Jack said.

Sam slowly got up from his bed and walked over to the bathroom. Jack followed closely behind. Both men stared at their reflections in the mirror in silence for a full two minutes until Sam finally spoke again.

"If that's really you in there, Simon," Sam began, his voice quivering with every syllable, "why do you look like that? How do I know it's even you in there?"

"I'm going to tell you everything I can remember, but first, there's something very important you need to know," Jack said.

"Which is?"

"I know how to reverse Periodic East."

"What the hell is Periodic East?"

"It's what caused the planet to go quiet. The consequence was the deaths of billions of people, a complete halt in communication. I should have done more to try to stop it. But I know how to make it right. I need you to help me do it."

"How?" Sam asked.

"We need to bring Icarus back to Earth."

TWENTY-FIVE

"*Leader?* So, their leader is nearby? How many more are there around here?" I asked, but Daniel was already asleep in a makeshift recliner. He needed the rest but no one else could communicate with the alien. It seemed docile enough; more curious than threatening, like how an old dog would react when a kitten is brought home.

The people that were with me were already starting to explore the subterranean civilization, though I still wasn't sure exactly how it got here. From the looks of it, it would've taken hundreds of people working around the clock to get something like this up and running. Or for all I knew, it was done by one alien in an instant; I just didn't know.

The alien walked around quietly watching everyone. After about an hour, everyone seemed to have come to the conclusion that it wasn't going to hurt us. Instead, it just seemed to want to study us.

I looked at the thermometer. It was seventy-four degrees Fahrenheit and everyone was just elated at peeling off layers of wet, stinky clothes and being comfortable again in what felt like years; and it had been. It seemed like whoever built this place wasn't here anymore and hadn't been for a long time. I settled into a room a little bigger than my bedroom on the ship. It even had some salvaged wood as a makeshift desk and a large pile of straw and banana leaves on the ground; a mattress. It was the epitome of luxury by anyone's standards these days.

I laid my pack on the table and started settling in when Sara walked in. She had a wide smile on her face as if she had been walking through Disneyland.

"Isn't this place amazing, Tiberius?" she asked.

"It is pretty amazing," I admitted.

"Can we stay here?" Sara asked, a large smile beaming across her face.

"I think we can stay here for now," I said, "but I don't know for how long. We will still need to go out and gather food again in the next day or so."

"But there's plenty of food in here. Oscar has a building that's just filled with bananas, figs, and even frozen meats on the other side of the cave."

"Oscar?" I repeated, confused.

"The alien; he looks like one of those old movie statues I saw in a book once," she said.

"Oscar…"

"Want to see the food building?"

"I'll go see it soon, Sara. Right now, I want to rest a little. I think that's what everyone is doing. Why don't you find Miles and take a nap? I think we all could use some comfortable sleep," I said, meaning every syllable of it.

Sara's face deflated in enthusiasm as she slowly walked away. I heard a faint "Okay," from her as she walked out of sight.

A few seconds later, I saw *Oscar* follow closely behind her. The alien seemed to be absolutely baffled by Sara. I hoped he wouldn't try to eat her, or worse.

I laid down on the mattress, and before I knew it, I was in a deep sleep. I had completely forgotten that sleep could feel this good.

When you don't have to worry about freezing to death every minute of every day, you immediately let your guard down, no matter how long you've had it up. It was exhausting to ensure that you didn't die of exhaustion.

I woke up to an unfamiliar sound. I had no idea how much time passed, but I was immediately in a state of panic as I got up from the makeshift mattress. Looking out, this place looked like impeccably preserved ancient ruins. Buildings were erected in minimalist design and style with what looked like laser precision. Each opening in a "room" gave a stunning panoramic view of the deep innards of the cave. I had no idea how deep the cave went, but from the looks of it, it would take me at least a day or two on foot to reach its end. I wondered if we were the only survivors here.

Looking through the "window," I saw Ada approaching me and I learned that the unfamiliar sound was her laughter. She approached in a jubilant outcry.

"Ada," I began, "are you alright? Did anything happen?"

"Tiberius, you have to come see," she started. "It's a miracle."

"What is?" I ask.

"It's Daniel," she began. I immediately cut her off.

"Is he okay? What happened?"

"Okay?" she began, "Didn't you hear what I said? It's a miracle. Come see."

I followed Ada back to the center of the cave. A crowd of all the survivors that followed me huddled around something, cheering. Some were even on their knees praying to something or someone that I couldn't see just yet.

"What's going on? Let me see," I said as I slithered my way to the front of the crowd.

When I was able to see what everyone was celebrating and praying over, I didn't know what to make of it. It wasn't

Oscar, but a young man that was probably in his twenties that I didn't recognize. Maybe another person made his way in here or he was the one who helped build this place.

The young man made eye contact with me and smiled wide.

"Tiberius," he gleefully shouted in a familiar voice.

"Do I know you?" I asked.

The young man smiled even wider before saying, "It's good, *Comandante*; it's good."

SIX
YEARS
AGO
(Part Four)

The Escape Pod...

TWENTY-SIX

The four men had entered a room about the size of a small walk-in closet. A sole console with only one large button was at the center. They all stared at the button momentarily in silence. Simon didn't know it yet, but the other three men, the three highest-ranking political figures left on the planet, knew exactly what it was. It was what would stop reality forever.

"What is this?" Simon asked.

"Don't ask questions, just be thankful," Vice President Sans snapped.

"Quiet, Patrick; show some respect," President Eastman snapped back.

Sans remained quiet and the four men continued to stare in silence for another minute.

"Mr. President," General Keats began, "you are the only person who can press that button, sir."

Eastman took a deep breath and looked over at Simon who hadn't made another sound and had barely been breathing.

"Simon," President Eastman began, "why don't you tell us a little about yourself."

Simon looked at him with confusion. "What would you like to know, Mr. President?"

"Well, first of all, you can drop the formalities. Call me Mike," he said with an exhausted smile. He then pointed to the Vice President before saying, "This is Patrick," and then pointing to General Keats, "and this is Frank."

"It's an honor to meet all of you," Simon said without remembering that he had met, seen, and even interacted with all three men almost daily.

Keats almost cracked a smile.

"Mike asked you a question, son."

"Right," Simon began, "I'm originally from New Orleans. I'm a true New Orleanian through and through. I studied at Loyola University."

"What about your family, Simon?" Eastman asked, "Where are they? Have you been able to contact any of them in the last few days?"

Simon sighed. "My sister died a few years ago in Scotland," he began, "parents also." A tear streamed down his face. "I have a brother—a twin—on Icarus."

Simon didn't think it was possible, but the room went even quieter than before. The four men looked at each other and then the button.

"You have a brother on Icarus?" the Vice President started. "Did I hear you right?"

"Yes, sir. Uh, yes, Patrick," Simon responded.

"Did you get to talk to him before he launched?" Keats asked.

"No, sir. I was… it's complicated, but I haven't seen or spoken to any of my family since I began this position. But he's the only surviving family I have left and I'd love to talk to him; just to let him know that I'm okay. For however much longer I have."

The President looked at the Vice President and top General and instantly made a decision. He started walking back the way he came with more determination than anyone had seen in some time.

"Come with me," Eastman said.

Simon followed behind and the other men started to

follow, but Eastman turned back and said, "You two stay here." He looked over at the Vice President and said, "I am resigning my position as President of the United States effective immediately and invoking the Twenty-fifth Amendment.

"You can't do that, Mike," Vice President Sans began, but Eastman kept talking.

"Don't interrupt me. I know that legally this is not how this is done, but who's going to argue? Right? You just said we won't have a history in the next few minutes anyways. I am going to take Simon somewhere classified—"

"Classified?" Keats repeated, "What are you talking about?"

"The escape pod," Eastman said. "I'm taking him to my pod. He's going to be the one to use it. Does anyone want to object? Go ahead and stop me."

The two other men just stared back blankly.

"Good," Eastman said and looked at Simon, "Come on."

✦

Michael Eastman and Simon Ng made their way back into the War Room and up the stairs and through the titanium doors back into the main ground floor of the White House. They hadn't seen any other person and didn't expect to. They went out of the Oval Office and into the President's Residency. Then, they made their way into the master bedroom.

"Help me with this," Eastman said as they both shifted the bed over. There, Simon saw an imprint of another opening.

"How many secret compartments and bunkers does this place have?"

"More than you'll ever know," Eastman said with a smile. "And this isn't a bunker," he began. "It's a spaceship."

"A what?" Simon asked.

"It has built-in coordinates to go straight to Icarus. No

matter what you touch on this thing, it won't deviate off course. You have water and food to last you a few weeks, maybe a month, if you ration smart, but I have no idea where Icarus is right now. You might make it. You might starve to death before it gets there. You might explode the minute this thing launches. You might get hit by space debris and explode then. I'm not trying to talk you out of this, I'm just telling you everything the engineers told me. They also told me that if there's a leak or failure in life support, you'll die. I can't calculate the exact probability of the success of this thing, but it's likely less than fifty percent."

"Why are you offering this to me, sir?" Simon asked.

President Eastman had tears building in his eyes. "I had to watch my family die," he began, "but at least I was with them in the end. You deserve to be with your family. And, if you're really lucky, you just might have a shot of a real future."

"Will Icarus know I'm coming?" Simon asked. "Is there any way that I can communicate with them en route?"

"No, and there's a reason for that. If they don't know you're coming, they won't have to decide whether or not to change course to try to intercept you and risk the lives of everyone on board. Also if you don't make it, no one, especially your brother, will be the wiser. But if you do make it, boy, what a story you'll tell. Keats and Sans are wrong; history *will* survive. And it will survive with *you*."

Eastman put his palm down again at the center of the opening and a panel slid open.

He looked at Simon and said, "It's your decision, son."

TWENTY-SEVEN

"The last thing I remember," Jack concluded, "was being inside the escape pod."

When he finished his story, Jack looked deep into Sam's eyes.

"This is impossible," Sam began. "What you're telling me happened six years ago. Even in hypersleep, you wouldn't have survived this long. And why do you look like that? You look nothing like Simon, and why identify yourself as Jack?" Sam rattled on, the tone in his voice matching the growing rage on his face. "You're not my brother," Sam concluded. "You're an imposter. You're a stowaway who has managed to sneak aboard Icarus only to fuck with my head." Sam pushed a button on his desk console. "Get out of my room and go fuck yourself."

"I can prove it," Jack said, "I can prove that I'm your brother. Take me to the ship's doctor; take my blood, plasma, DNA sample, whatever. I can't explain why I look different—maybe they can—but, surely, they can show that I'm still your brother."

"Was I dreaming?" Sam asked.

"What?"

"The first night I saw you, on the Bridge, was that you?"

"Yeah, that was me," Jack said, confused.

"So, why is it that I suddenly woke up in my bed?

Huh? Why was the ship empty? Why were all the coolers in the Mess Hall empty? Huh? Why did you have a gun?"

"The gun was with me in the escape pod. I bet if we found that pod, we'd have loads of answers," Jack interrupted.

"How the fuck do I know I'm not the one going crazy right now? How do I know that you're even real?" Sam's voice boomed throughout his room as Jack stared silently wishing he had more answers.

"Take me to the doctor, Sam. Let them prove that I am who I say I am," Jack began, "and maybe you should get yourself checked out also. I mean when was the last time you slept? When was the last time you really remember having a good night's sleep? I told you the last thing I remembered. What's the last thing that *you* remember?"

Sam looked at the surface of his nightstand and pushed a small button on the side, which caused a drawer to pop open. From the drawer, he took out a small picture frame of himself with Simon dating back over fifteen years ago. The person in the picture looked like a slightly younger version of the Simon that had been with President Eastman in the White House. Sam stared at it for a moment, then slid it over to Jack.

"That's my brother, Simon," Sam said as his voice lowered with each syllable. "He was smart; really smart. Since he was seven or eight years old, he was determined to work in the White House. I know that because he told me. You want to prove to me you're my brother, tell me why. Why did he want to work for the White House?"

Jack looked at the photo and tears started streaming down his face. He smiled looking at a photo in a setting that he had not remembered, but it was Samuel and Simon Ng in that photo together.

"He—I" Jack began, choking up. "I wanted to find aliens for the government."

More tears streamed down Sam's face at the correct

response.

 "And I did, Sam. I did."

TWENTY-EIGHT

I couldn't believe my eyes. Daniel was no longer eighty-four. He looked twenty-four. His piercing green eyes and his voice, though much more youthful-sounding, were still the same. The people that remained in our camp marveled and looked towards the alien—or Oscar as Sara had named him—who was standing about fifty feet back observing and began making their way towards him. They were chanting, praying, declaring Oscar a god. Some even fell to their knees and tried to kiss his odd-looking feet.

But Oscar was completely confused by this reaction and continued taking steps backward trying to avoid any contact with any of us.

"Wait!" I called out as I looked at Daniel who was still marveling at his new self. "Let's have Daniel ask him why he did this," I said.

"He do it so we can talk longer, Tiberius," Daniel said walking as if he literally had springs attached to each step.

"Is that what he told you?" I asked. "He did this to you to keep you alive longer?"

"Yes, I suppose," Daniel began. "He must be lonely; no one here to talk to him for a long time."

"How long? Ask him how long he's been here," I said.

Daniel approached Oscar, pleading the rest of the people to stay back and give them some room.

"*Noiztik zaude hemen?*"

Oscar looked directly at a now-youthful Daniel with an expression as if he really had to think about it, or maybe try to understand the question—I didn't know. Eventually, Oscar answered.

"Beti egon naiz hemen."

"He say, 'always,' Tiberius. He say he here always."

I wasn't sure the alien, or Oscar, truly understood what Daniel was asking it. I suddenly remembered as he looked directly into my eyes that I needed to ask again about their leader and why he killed Joshua. I turned to Daniel who was continuing to marvel at his younger self with a wide smile on his face. I approached Daniel with a slight smile myself.

"Daniel," I began, "it's great to see you like this."

"Yes, Tiberius," he said. "Now, I younger than you."

"That's true. You certainly look younger than me now," I said. He looked not only sixty years younger, but in prime physical shape as well.

"I feel brand new," he said. "I feel alive."

Sitting with the group, a thought entered my head and I was almost mad at myself for not thinking this sooner. I looked around at what other people from our group were still with us and confirmed my theory.

"I know why the alien did what he did for you and no one else," I said quietly to Daniel. "You're the only person who speaks his language. The alien wants you to have more time to teach others your language so more can communicate with it and probably even procreate. I was right. You are the most important person on the planet."

I wasn't sure if Daniel fully understood everything I said. I knew he didn't understand the word 'procreate.' But I didn't want to dumb it down for him just yet. I still needed to know who Oscar's leader was and why they killed Joshua.

"Come with me, Daniel," I said.

Daniel followed closely behind as he marveled at his surroundings as if he were seeing them for the first time. I guess it's understandable to assume that his eyesight wasn't so great either.

Daniel kept whispering, "Wow," to himself as we made our way to Oscar, who was standing at a distance from the rest of the group, who had decided to construct a makeshift shrine to it from their own personal items.

I approached Oscar slowly with Daniel next to me.

"I need to ask you something important," I began.

I looked at Daniel to translate for me and he did. Oscar looked at Daniel for translation after I spoke and then to me again after Daniel translated awaiting my questions.

"Why would your leader kill? Your leader killed a member of my camp. Why?"

Oscar looked at Daniel again for translation and as Daniel translated I saw the expression on Oscar's face change ever so slightly. After a few agonizing seconds of waiting for his answer, Oscar's voice reverberated through the cavern walls again.

"*Gu hiltzen saiatzen dena baino ez dugu hiltzen. Guru buruzagiak erabakitzen du hoiz hil.*"

I looked at Daniel to translate.

"He say they kill only when someone try to kill them first. Only leader decide when to kill."

If that were true, I certainly wouldn't have put it past Joshua to not be entirely truthful about his initial encounter when he found the other alien. Who knew how Joshua tried to thaw out the alien or even if it had been frozen in the first place. For all we knew… Well, it didn't matter anymore.

"Are we safe here?" I asked Oscar and then repeated the question again to Daniel to translate, which he did. Oscar then responded again immediately and Daniel said that we were indeed safe.

After about another hour of questioning, Daniel, myself, and the rest of us learned a few more important things about this place.

There were a few geysers in the cavern that provided all the water we would ever need for drinking, and it also explained why the cavern was so much warmer than any other place we'd experienced since The Blast. It was also a great spot for cooking and bathing. A large shed that had been built to store food already had enough to maintain a group of our size for weeks, but we were, of course, free to go out of the cave to find more food when we needed it, or we could even leave if we wanted to. We were not by any means being held captive.

One of the buildings even had a room filled with hand-written journals, which I was immediately drawn to.

As I flipped through the pages of the journals, I saw that they were written in various languages including English, Spanish, French, Dutch, and Japanese, just to name a few. Miles poured through the Dutch journal and I went through the English. Daniel said he would look through the Spanish and French ones later. He was too busy enjoying his newfound youth.

The journals I read dated back to just weeks after The Blast. The author documented how he found the cave with his own group of survivors and the "giant saints" inside. "Saints," as in more than one. It didn't specify if this particular survivor left or why. He could've died from going out looking for supplies one day, which was certainly possible.

I tried really hard not to jump to conclusions of betrayal or double-crossing. Miles told me similar things were written from the Dutch journal he read. The entries also suddenly stopped without explanation or even warning of something bad happening within days of each other. Again, the possibility that they could've suddenly died while out looking for food occurred to me. The last entries from each journal were two days apart, just under four years. Back then, there were a lot more starving and desperate survivors and a lot more starving and desperate animals that could've easily killed them.

Two days went by. Oscar, for the most part, ignored us as we adjusted to this new, better way of life. No one ever saw Oscar sleep, but he would sit just outside one particular building like an old man from the Bayou and watch us like a nosy neighbor who saw new people moving in the neighborhood. I wondered what he was guarding in that building.

The following morning, Miles came by to schedule a time for us to go out to gather more food and supplies. As we were putting together a schedule, Daniel walked in. His new appearance was something that we all were still getting used to.

"I go with you," Daniel began, "I young and strong now. I help."

Miles and I looked at each other silently and weighed our options with our facial expressions. We could certainly use the extra set of hands and energy, but we didn't want to run the risk of Daniel getting hurt or worse out there. Yes, he was young, but he wasn't immortal. At least, we didn't think so. We still needed someone to be able to communicate with Oscar for when we had more questions or needed more information.

"Tell you what," Miles began, "I'll go with you to gather more plantain leaves and fruit, but we can't go more than half a kilometer out."

Miles looked at me for approval as he said it and I nodded slightly. When Miles saw my signal, he continued, "But, Daniel, I don't want you climbing any trees. Just pick up the stuff you can reach or is already on the ground, deal?"

Daniel smiled his amazing new smile. "Okay, Miles. I help out."

As the three of us were finalizing a schedule, Ada walked by. She made eye contact with Daniel and winked at him. Daniel winked back and looked at Miles and I.

"We don't leave right now, yes?" Daniel asked as Miles and I tried to hold back our laughter.

"No, Daniel," Miles said.

"Not just yet," I confirmed.

"You come find me when you ready, okay?"

"Okay," Miles and I both said in unison and, in an instant, Daniel had run off to join Ada on her walk.

TWENTY-NINE

Icarus had its own hospital, where members of the crew were treated for everything from the sniffles, to on-the-job injuries, to cancer—the cure for which had been discovered nine years before. The hospital consisted of seven doctors varying in different disciplines and specialties, and luckily, no deaths or severe injuries had yet occurred.

There was a very specific reason as to why there were an odd number of doctors on Icarus. Much like the Supreme Court of the United States—back when there was one—any disagreements or debates over the best course of action when treating a patient could never end in a tie. In all the time since Icarus's launch, no such disputes had ever occurred.

Sam and Jack entered the north wing of Icarus to a set of double doors that simply said "Hospital" as they walked in. To greet them was Dr. Reynolds, a pediatrician who often doubled as the hospital's receptionist.

"Good morning, Sam," he said with bubbly enthusiasm, perfect for someone who worked exclusively with children. He then looked closer at Jack and seemed a little confused.

"What can I do for you two today? Or maybe you just came by for one of my specialty lollipops?"

"No," Sam said as he laid his hands on the table and

leaned forward. "I need you guys to run a DNA test."

Dr. Reynolds looked at Jack more closely and tried to discreetly look through his database, but Sam saved him the trouble.

"You won't find him in your records, Doc, or any records," Sam began. "That's why I need you to run a DNA test, and add him to the ship's database.

Dr. Reynolds was taken aback. "I can't just… Where did this… Who is this person?" Dr. Reynolds finally blurted out, but before Sam or Jack could answer, Dr. Reynolds kept talking. "I can add a baby on the ship's database, but not an adult. How did he get on board? Who is he?"

"That's what the DNA test is for," Jack said, startling Dr. Reynolds. "It's to prove that I'm Samuel Ng's twin brother."

"You don't need a doctor," Dr. Reynolds said to Sam, "You need security. You also need to inform Captain Bellamy and Dr. Miyaki if you haven't done so already. In fact, let me do that for you,"

"No!" Jack yelled as Dr. Reynolds started pushing a few buttons on his desk console. This reaction also surprised Sam.

"He's right," Sam began. "We have to inform the Captain of your arrival anyways. I just thought," Sam continued as he now was looking at Dr. Reynolds, "that I could confirm who he is before I tell the Captain of his being on board."

"Are you listening to yourself, Sam? You need to get out of this hospital and inform the Captain immediately. If you don't, I will," Dr. Reynolds said, forcefully.

Sam suddenly had a change of heart and a realization when he said, "Before I inform the Captain, I want to be able to prove to her who this person is. How long does it take to run a DNA test?"

Dr. Reynolds stared intently at them both as other doctors started to peek their heads out of their offices and examination rooms.

"How long?" Sam asked again.

"About thirty seconds," Dr. Reynolds answered sheepishly.

"Get one of those tests and confirm for me that a miracle has occurred and I have here a member of my family I haven't seen in over ten years. Now!" Sam demanded.

Dr. Reynolds got up from his desk and said, "Wait here."

He stepped into his office momentarily and came back out with a digital pad and a device used to gather and analyze blood. It was a cylindrical tube with a syringe on one end and a button on the other. He looked at both Simon and Jack and took a deep breath. "Left arm, please," he said in a monotone voice as Jack stood up and extended his left arm.

Dr. Reynolds quickly injected Jack and held the cylindrical syringe in Jack's arm for about twenty seconds. Jack's blood began to fill the syringe as the tube itself began to alternate colors like a disco ball. Once filled, the tube turned a bright white.

Dr. Reynolds then referenced his digital pad. "This is the ship's database," he explained as he was looking at Sam. "It has everyone's DNA signature on file. If this is your twin brother, the signature will be nearly identical to yours and it will tell me if there is a blood relation. It'll just take another moment."

Jack sat down and Sam felt the moment pass at an agonizingly slow speed. He continued to stare at Jack the entire time and Jack looked at Dr. Reynolds intensely.

"The results are in," Dr. Reynolds said suddenly, and his expression confirmed the results. "The man sitting next to you, Sam," he began, "is your twin brother."

Sam's reaction was as if he were experiencing the five

stages of grief in his head simultaneously. He thought he'd be happy about it, but, deep down, he wasn't. He couldn't understand why. Maybe it was because this Jack person looked nothing like Simon. Sam was also confused over how no one else on the ship before this moment seemed to have noticed or questioned him. Even if he had arrived just a few days before, surely someone must've noticed him.

"Now kindly leave the hospital and report to Captain Bellamy and Dr. Miyaki immediately," Dr. Reynolds said suddenly again as Sam was continuing to go through this impossible scenario in his head.

"SIS," Sam began, "where are Captain Bellamy and Kairi Miyaki?"

Those muted clicks again, "Captain Bellamy and Dr. Kairi Miyaki are both in Dr. Kairi Miyaki's quarters."

Sam looked at Jack—Simon—and stood up. "Follow me," he said. "I have so many more questions that you need to answer."

He knew that with the sudden and mysterious appearance of a new person on Icarus without anyone's knowledge for sure Kairi and Captain Bellamy would be convinced that a MAC scrub would be necessary.

THIRTY

It was the first time Sam had been inside Kairi's quarters since he spent the night with her. Even though it had only been a few nights before, for Sam, it felt like it had been hours.

As Sam and Simon were walking through the halls of Icarus, they passed other members of the crew who were poorly trying to hide their stares. Sam noticed that most of the stares were directed at him and not the new fully-formed adult that found his way on board still without explanation. He ignored this realization and explained it away in his mind by concluding that it was just slight paranoia brought on by tremendous amounts of stress. Stress was absolutely warranted in his mind.

Both men reached the door to Kairi's quarters and Sam took a deep breath before speaking.

"These two are the most important and powerful people on board Icarus," he began. "What I'm about to ask of them has never been asked before by anyone and it's going to be the second time I ask it. Treat them both courteously and respectfully. Do you understand?"

Simon nodded. "I understand you, Sam," he said with a tone of familiarity that made Sam uncomfortable. "I don't exactly understand what you're going to ask of them, but I know it must be important and that it's the right thing to do. I know that because I know you."

The last remark made Sam particularly uncomfortable.

"Before we go in," Sam said, "I know you can't explain why you look like that, but why do you insist on being called Jack? If you are Simon—"

"I know what you're saying," Simon interrupted. "But the truth of the matter is, I don't recognize *Simon* looking like this. I am him but—"

"Wouldn't that be the first step towards recognizing and accepting… this?" Sam asked while gesturing with his arms over Simon's—Jack's—appearance. "To go by your given name. I think it would also help make my—our—case when we go in there and ask this impossible ask," Sam concluded, raising an excellent point, which caused Simon to sigh deeply.

"Okay," he began. "You're right. I am and always will be Simon, no matter what I look like."

Sam smiled and placed his hand on his brother's shoulder. "Come on, Simon," Sam said. "Let's figure out how you got here."

✦

Sam pushed a button just outside Kairi's quarters; a doorbell, as it were. Without any response, the doors swung open. Inside, Kairi's quarters were just as Sam remembered it. Why would it be any different? Immaculately kept and minimally decorated. In the common area sat Kairi and Captain Bellamy, neither one looked up from their reading material as both gentlemen walked in.

Sam audibly cleared his throat before speaking. "I'm sorry to bother you," he began, "but I'm glad you're both here because I need to speak to both of you."

Captain Bellamy looked up from her reading material and saw Sam and the unfamiliar man standing beside him. She did her best to keep her poker face, but could immediately tell that the man next to Sam was someone that she had never seen before.

"Yes," she began. "Dr. Miyaki and I were just about to have some tea. Would you care to join us?"

"That's very kind of you," Simon interjected, startling Captain Bellamy a little more. "We'd love to."

"Dr. Miyaki," Captain Bellamy began. "Would you please set up two more place settings for Sam and—"

"Simon," he said. "My name is Simon."

Kairi finally looked up from her reading material and barely flinched at seeing the two men, one of whom, of course, was a complete stranger. She simply stood up and looked at Captain Bellamy. "Of course, Captain," she said and made her way into the kitchen.

"Sit, both of you, please, " Captain Bellamy said. "Sam, I wanted to let you know that I just reviewed your monthly report," she said, trying to sound cavalier. "Good work," she concluded.

"Thank you, Captain," Sam replied as both men sat on the semicircular sofa in Kairi's common room; a round coffee table, in a muted color, at the center.

Dr. Miyaki emerged from the kitchen with a round tray that had four tea cups and a teapot in the center and laid it on the coffee table before sitting down.

"So, who's this?" Kairi asked in her usual unabashed way.

"This is Simon," Sam began. "Simon Ng; my twin brother."

Both women looked at Simon closely and were speechless.

"I don't understand," Captain Bellamy began.

"Fraternal," Sam interjected quickly, "but clearly even that is hard to believe and the last question on your minds right now."

"The doctor just completed a DNA test," Simon said

respectfully. "I think he said he was going to send you both the results as we made our way over here."

Both women looked at their portable screens and saw a notification of a new member on board Icarus, only it wasn't a birth. Without knowing how else to declare him, Dr. Reynolds had labeled Simon as a "Stowaway."

Kairi looked up from her screen at Simon and stared him down. Truly, this was something to behold when Dr. Kairi Miyaki, one of the most brilliant minds to ever live, was stumped and speechless. Captain Bellamy immediately noticed, which diminished her poker face.

"Simon," Captain Bellamy said.

"Yes, Captain?" Simon responded with utmost respect and poise.

"What are you doing on board Icaurs? *How* did you get on board Icarus?" Captain Bellamy asked.

"I was sent here by President Michael Eastman on his escape pod. He sacrificed himself so that I could hopefully be reunited with my brother. That's really all I remember. I—"

"President Eastman?" Kairi interrupted. "He was the president who—"

"Dr. Mikyaki, please," Captain Bellamy said quickly and authoritatively to cut her off.

"Mr. Ng—Simon Ng—I'm sure you have many questions that need answers, but so do I. Where is the escape pod now?"

"I wish I knew, Captain. I have no memory of the last… my last memory was being launched in that escape pod; when Operation Periodic East was initiated," Simon said.

"Operation Periodic East? What does that have to do with you being here now?" Kairi asked.

"It's a long story."

"You have no recollection as to when you arrived?"

"Recent memory; nothing past the last day or two,"

Simon answered, almost ashamed.

Simon calmly explained everything he had explained to Sam; the last of what he remembered. He told her about his work with President Eastman and believing to be the first person to intercept First Contact before General Keats broadcasted it publicly to the world. Then, he told her about how, three hours later, he initiated Operation Periodic East, severing all forms of modern communication.

It was Keats who ultimately pressed the button.

"All the reports I've read on Operation Periodic East were deemed inconclusive and speculation at best," Kairi argued.

"Well, I saw it happen," Simon said. "After President Eastman's pod successfully launched with me inside," he continued, "I received a call on a portable communicator inside the escape pod. It seemed like the other men didn't know Eastman had made the call so I stayed quiet. I saw Eastman back in that secret bunker behind the War Room. Eastman looked like a shell of himself. 'This is so history will remember,' Eastman whispered. The three men stared at the button and after about two minutes of what I thought was a lost connection because everyone was so still and quiet, Keats just smashed the button. The call disconnected a few seconds later."

As he said all this, Simon reached into his pockets and took out a charred portable communicator that looked beyond repair.

"If you can fix this," Simon began, "you can see for yourself."

Immediately, Kairi lunged for the device and took it from Simon's hands. Sam looked over to Captain Bellamy who was in a quiet state of shock over what she had just heard. She was processing everything—the way a good Captain would, and she was the best.

"Captain," Sam said, "I must request again that Icarus

undergo a MAC scrub. Doing so will not only help determine how and when Simon arrived, but also—"

"Yes," she suddenly replied and then looked over to Kairi. As the Captain stood up, everyone followed suit.

"Prepare the initial procedures for a MAC scrub," Captain Bellamy said. "I will alert the crew and instruct them to prepare to re-enter a hypersleep state. I want it to begin as soon as possible."

Kairi still had her never-before-seen speechless look on her face. She seemed vulnerable and human.

"Yes, Captain Bellamy," she replied softly. "Right away."

Kairi walked out of her own quarters leaving the Captain, Sam, and Simon in the room.

THIRTY-ONE

Daniel, Miles, and I returned from our supply excursion. I could tell he was a little restless, but Daniel kept his word about only foraging what he could reach and not climbing any tree or reaching for a fruit dangling from a branch off a cliff. Our haul was honestly not nearly as much as we usually gathered, but our group was also far fewer in numbers. We honestly still had supplies to last us for weeks, and with our new living conditions vastly improved, morale had skyrocketed.

While we were out, we were told by Ada, Sara, and a few others that Oscar remained mostly silent and docile. People were leaving gifts of pelt, candy, and personal items outside the building in the cavern that he usually hung around.

When Oscar saw that we had returned, he made a beeline for Daniel. Oscar's voice echoed off the cavernous walls. Daniel replied in his native tongue and Oscar remained still and silent. He then made a one-syllable sound, turned, and continued his random pacing around the cavern.

I asked Daniel what they talked about, and Daniel just said that Oscar had asked where we were and why we had left. Daniel gave his answer of searching for food and what humans needed to survive. The one-syllable response from Oscar that ended the conversation loosely translated to "I see."

✦

Things were great. They really were. We had all been here just over a week. The space was more than ample; enough for all of us and more. We started designating and decorating certain buildings for certain purposes.

One was converted into a school for Sara and the few other children that made their way to the cave with us.

Another building was converted into a crafting station for Ada, who I had just found out was a textiles artist from Ukraine. Daniel had personally taken it upon himself to help her design it however she wanted. Miles claimed the building across from the one that was designated as the school for him and Sara. Daniel chose the building between Ada's studio and where Oscar was. I stayed at a building on the edge of the cavern close to the geysers. Who would have thought that I would miss humidity that much? I unpacked my personal items and arranged them exactly as I had them on the boat, but this space was now nearly four times the size. It felt enormous.

One morning, we woke up to find Oscar was gone. Everyone was unsure over how to react to his absence. A few people suggested that Daniel go out and look for him. Some worried that we had done something to anger or offend him. Some were also secretly relieved that Oscar had left.

"Did Oscar tell you he was leaving or when he'd be back?" I asked Daniel, already knowing the answer.

"Oscar tell me nothing, Tiberius," Daniel responded with a confused tone.

"Did he mention that he wanted or needed something in the last few days that maybe you forgot?" Miles asked as we all tried to think of a rhyme or reason why the alien suddenly vanished without a trace.

"I don't remember," Daniel admitted to Miles, almost ashamed of the response.

"Maybe he left a note," Sara suddenly chimed in. "Don't people sometimes leave notes saying where they went or when they'll be back?"

"Oscar isn't a *person*," I said to Sara, which caused her to give me a look of utter confusion.

Suddenly, Daniel did remember something from what Sara said. "A note," he said with a loud whisper. "He did say something to me soon after we arrive," Daniel began. "Oscar talk to me about what is best way to message everyone and I say to write a note and I read and translate."

"So you're saying he might have left us a note somewhere in here?" Miles asked.

"Maybe," Daniel said with new youthful exuberance. "I find it and translate," he concluded.

"We'll all look," I said, looking around at the group that gathered. "If you find a note somewhere, just shout."

We all dispersed to find a note that we didn't know for certain existed. The first place to obviously look was the building that Oscar spent the majority of his time in. No one had ever seen the inside. Daniel and Ada were the ones to enter first. It was filled with items that seemed from another world; things that they nor anyone else had ever seen before that neither one of them could make heads or tails of. They called for the rest of us to come see.

Inside Oscar's building were bright, metallic objects that ranged in size from something that would fit in the palm of your hand to a six-foot person. We were all apprehensive about touching or even getting too close to any of these things.

There was still a possibility that Oscar would return at any second, see us all rummaging through the alien technology, and kill us all on sight. All of a sudden, I started to get nervous.

"Miles," I pulled aside, "why don't you wait outside and see if Oscar suddenly returns."

Miles knew what I was getting at and reluctantly nodded and quietly made his way outside as everyone else kept looking around at a loss for words.

"Daniel, did Oscar ever tell you anything about what he did before we arrived?" I asked.

"No, Tiberius," Daniel replied.

"Maybe it's not in here," I concluded. "Or maybe it is and no one here knows the first thing about finding it. I mean it's not like he would just spray paint it on the back of a random building, right?"

"Tiberius! Daniel!" Miles suddenly shouted from a distance. "you need to come see this. Now!" he continued as we all rushed out and followed the sound of Miles's voice.

We stopped outside the back of Daniel's building where we saw another alien metallic object at Miles's feet that was a powerful makeshift projector of sorts. A beam of light shot out of this little device that expanded into a projection that took up an entire ten-foot wall.

We all looked at Daniel in desperation to translate and Daniel just squinted at it as he was still adjusting to having a young man's vision again. Daniel stayed completely silent except for the faintest of whispers I heard from him. I assumed he was reading the note to himself over and over.

It was an agonizing few silent minutes until Sara broke it. "What does it say?" Sara asked. "When is Oscar coming back?"

"It say," Daniel began, "that he feel something."

"Oscar?" Sara confirmed. "Like sick?"

"Yes… I don't know… Something different that Oscar never feel before."

"Is this 'feeling' described?" I asked.

Daniel was quiet as he mouthed a portion of the projected note to himself again before he answered.

"More," Daniel said.

"More? More what?" Miles asked.

"It—I no sure. It just say, 'I feel something more. I go find more.'"

"More food?" Sara asked.

"More people?" Miles suggested.

"More beings like him?" I asked, looking Daniel in the eyes.

"I sorry, Tiberius. It just say 'more.'"

✦

✦

BASQUE TRANSLATIONS

Bakarrik zaude? — Are you alone?

Ez nago bakarrik. Zuregana etorriko gara. — I am not alone. We will come to you.

Nor zara? — Who are you?

Zure motako zenbat daude? — How many of your kind are there?

Askoz gehiago. — Many more.

Kobazuloan al daude? — Are they in the cave?

Hainbat lekutan. — Different places.

Jarraitu. — Continue.

Zein da zure izena? — What is your name?

Nire izena da... — My name is...

Ez dakit... Ahaztu egin zait. — I don't know... I forgot.

Ez dut hiltzen. — I don't kill.

Ez dut hiltzen, gure buruzagiak egiten du. — I do not kill, but our leader does.

Noiztik zaude hemen? — How long have you been here?

Beti egon naiz hemen. — I have always been here.

Gu hiltzen saiatzen dena baino ez dugu hiltzen. Guru buruzagiak erabakitzen du hoiz hil. — We only kill someone when they are trying to kill us. Our leader decides when to kill.

Turn the page for an excerpt from
Gabriel L. Rodríguez's second installment
in the *Periodic East* series

PARALLAX

Book Two

Coming 2024

ONE

Dr. Kairi Miyaki stormed out of her quarters, a decision that was not her own. She didn't bother waiting for people to get out of her way and knocked down a small child as she blindly turned a corner. She didn't stop or apologize. With each step she took, Kairi's stride got a little faster until she was in a full-on sprint.

Kairi was furious for multiple reasons. On the one hand, the very notion of a failure or oversight to her design of Icarus's Symbiotic Icarus System (SIS) was embarrassing. On the other, the very real threat of a new person on board was supposed to be impossible.

The thought of failure, a human certainty, made Kairi especially mad. If an entire person can make it on board undetected, then why not two? Or worse, a microscopic threat. She couldn't worry about that. That's what the Malfunctions Access Computations, or MAC, scrub was for. To figure those things out. Kairi was on her way to begin a process that would take hours to complete. A MAC scrub had only been done once; right before Icarus launched six years prior. And back then, the crew didn't have to be ordered to prepare to go into hypersleep.

An alert sounded in every personal quarters and common area to ensure that every person onboard Icarus heard the announcement simultaneously.

Captain Katherine Bellamy was still in Kairi's personal quarters with ship Liaison Samuel Ng and the "stowaway," genetically confirmed—despite no resemblance—to be Sam's twin brother, Simon, a man who mysteriously arrived onboard with no recollection of how or when he got there.

"Citizens of Icarus," Captain Bellamy's voice reverberated through every square inch of the space station as Kairi zig-zagged her way through the halls and into the Main Engineering section of the station, "A phenomenon has occurred on board that requires the most immediate and thorough investigation. A MAC scrub will be initiated as soon as possible."

As soon as Captain Bellamy announced the MAC scrub, the residents in the common areas shared looks of shock, confusion, and anxiety.

The Captain continued, "I want to reassure everyone on board that there is no threat to our life support or safety. The reasons for this order will be revealed to all citizens when we have the appropriate information to share. Report to your assigned hypersleep pods at zero-five hundred hours."

"Zero-five hundred," Kairi repeated to herself as she began the MAC scrub initiation. A process that can best be compared to depressurizing a submarine; something that, within itself, takes a lot of time.

"All infants will be in the same hypersleep pods as their mothers and we have additional pods if needed," Captain Bellamy continued. "Dr. Miyaki or I will provide any updates and information as needed. We thank you for your patience and cooperation regarding this most unusual situation. More answers are forthcoming. Captain out."

Captain Bellamy took a deep breath, the final sound that decrescendoed the alert that faded to silence. She stayed silent looking at the two men as if lost in thought.

"Thank you, Captain," Sam finally spoke.

Captain Bellamy simply gave a nervous smile before an alert of a personal call came into Kairi's quarters. It was

Kairi herself calling from Main Engineering.

"MAC scrub has been initiated, Captain. Life support will be turned off and the scrub will begin at zero-five hundred hours as you announced. That's in ten hours."

"Thank you, Dr. Miyaki," Captain Bellamy said. "Once you finish, please take some personal time."

"Thank you, Captain. But I don't think I will be able to."

"Neither will I, Kairi. Neither will I…"

The call disconnected leaving them in awkward silence again for a few moments before Simon spoke.

"Captain," Simon began. "Thank you. I—I want answers just as bad as you do. So, thank you."

"You're welcome, Simon," Captain Bellamy began. "You've never been through a MAC scrub and I don't know what you know about hypersleep, so let me walk you through it. A MAC scrub is the most sophisticated self-diagnostic system in existence. Icarus will completely shut down. Life support, secondary power, everything. There is a small satellite orbiting Icarus whose sole purpose is to scan the entire station as well as look for any phenomenon, like your pod, within Icarus's orbit within the last two years. I just hope you haven't been hiding on board for longer than that."

"I doubt that myself, Captain," Simon responded.

"The hypersleep pods are self-containing," Captain Bellamy continued, "which means that they operate on their own power source independent from that of Icarus. That's how we stay alive inside them. They will administer a powerful, yet one hundred percent safe gas within the chamber, which will put us in a sleep-like state for up to sixty hours. The MAC scrub will take thirty."

"Why does hypersleep last twice as long as the MAC scrub itself?" Sam asked.

"It takes time for all the systems within the ship to

power-up properly. This way when the crew wakes up hungry and a little disoriented, they won't have to wait to get whatever they need."

"I understand," Simon said.

"Me too," Sam added.

"We still have ten hours, gentlemen," Captain Bellamy began. "I encourage you both to spend time together in Sam's quarters. Catch up. Maybe you can even remember how you got here."

"Yes, Captain. Thank you," Sam responded.

"Captain, I have a question," Simon interjected.

"Please, go ahead."

"This satellite that performs the actual MAC scrub, can it receive signals, too? Can it communicate with Earth?"

"It can," Captain Bellamy responded, somewhat perplexed. "Although Icarus has never heard a response. We know that only a handful of survivors remain on Earth, but we have no idea what condition they are in. Physically or mentally."

"Did Icarus ever make it to Mars as it had intended to? Why wasn't it ever inhabited? And why did you come back while," Simon looked out the window and stared at Earth, "while being so close to home?"

Captain Bellamy rose from the semi-circular sofa. "Gentlemen, if you'll excuse me. I have a lot of work to do. Sam, please show your brother around the ship. He has a lot to learn about his new home."

"Yes, Captain," Sam replied as Captain Bellamy made her way toward the door without looking back. She walked out of Dr. Miyaki's personal quarters in silence, leaving behind all of Simon's unanswered questions.

ACKNOWLEDGMENTS

There are so many people to thank and I know I can't name them all individually. First and foremost, thank you to my wife, Katherine, for always being my number one fan.

I want to thank my parents for always being a bottomless well of ideas and inspiration simply by being in their presence.

To my best friends in "The Cabbage Patch" groupchat (Adrian, Alex, Zisko, Joel, and Cantero), thank you for the words of encouragement and support over the years.

Thank you to all my teachers and professors who motivated and inspired me to keep going with my crazy stories, particularly my mentor Robert Keats, who I know is smiling down on me from the next life.

My dear friend, Dr. Rahul Patel, thank you for being my science advisor on this project.

Thank you to my editor, Flor Ana Mireles, for your endless patience and enthusiasm in working with me on this project, and my other editor, Enrico Botha, for being so enthusiastic from the very first draft of this crazy thing.

Thank you to my students for constantly asking for updates on my projects over the years and for allowing me to go off on tangents as I explain them. (It's particularly great when I can actually segue them into the day's lesson.)

Thank you to Matteo Guarnieri, for creating the amazing artworks that are the front and back covers of the book and to Anirban Chakraborty, the interior illustrations artist.

I also want to thank Larraitz Ariznabarreta of the Center for Basque Studies at the University of Nevada, Reno for helping us with all the translations of a dying but beautiful language.

Thank you, Sarah Whalen, for taking my author photo.

Thank you to all the authors and readers who were granted early access to my book that contributed to the blurbs and praise—JP, KaliVictoria, Vincent, Cecilia, Katherine, Eva, Alexandrea, Melissa, Marcela, and Maria Jose.

Thank you to Indie Earth Publishing for having such faith in me from the very beginning.

Last but not least, thank **you, reader**. Thank you for taking the time to go on this crazy ride. I hope you enjoy it and know that more is to come if you do.

ABOUT THE AUTHOR

Gabriel L. Rodríguez was born and raised in Miami, Florida. From a young age, he was fascinated by movies, video games, comic books, and any other form of storytelling he could get his hands on. He majored in English at Florida International University in Miami, where he got his Bachelors, and then went to film school where he got a Masters in Motion Picture and Television with a screenwriting focus at The Academy of Art University in San Francisco.

Gabriel has always gotten inspiration for his stories from the most unlikely places; a stain on the floor, a family pet, or last night's leftovers.

Today, Gabriel works as a teacher in Miami, Florida, where he teaches Creative Writing, Film, Theory of Knowledge, and is the Advisor for the school literary magazine. He also enjoys traveling with his wife, Katherine, and having not-so-one-sided conversations with their cat, Lola.

Instagram: @GLRAuthor

ABOUT THE PUBLISHER

Indie Earth Publishing is an independent, author-first co-publishing company based in Miami, FL, dedicated to giving authors and writers the creative freedom they deserve. Indie Earth combines the freedom of self-publishing with the support and backing of traditional publishing for poetry, fiction, and short story collections by providing a plethora of services meant to aid them in the book publishing experience.

With Indie Earth Publishing, you are more than just another author, you are part of the Indie Earth creative family, making a difference one book at a time.

www.indieearthbooks.com

For inquiries, please email:
indieearthpublishinghouse@gmail.com

Instagram: @indieearthbooks

9 798986 989129